THE OK TEAM

NICK PLACE

ALLEN&UNWIN

First published in 2008

Allen & Unwin
83 Alexander St
Crows Nest NSW 2065
Australia
Phone: (61 2) 8425 0100
Fax: (61 2) 9906 2218
Email: info@allenandunwin.com
Web: www.allenandunwin.com

National Library of Australia
Cataloguing-in-Publication entry:
    Place, Nick, 1965- .
    The ok team.

    For children.
    ISBN 9781741751864 (pbk.).

    1. Heroes - Australia - Juvenile fiction. I. Title.

A823.4

Cover and text design by Josh Durham, Design by Committee
Cover and text illustrations by Heath McKenzie
Cover and text hero photographs from bigstockphoto.com and istockphoto.com
Chapter opening photographs by Nick Place
Set in 11.5/14.8pt Baskerville by Midland Typesetters, Australia
Printed in Australia by McPherson's Printing Group

10 9 8 7 6 5 4 3 2 1

www.herohints.com

Again, to Wonder Anna, the amazing flame-haired super-heroine.
And to the Fitzroy Hero Development Squad:
Lightning Rod and the Boy Who Moves the Stars.
Whatever superpowers I do possess can never be enough.

CONTENTS

CHAPTER 1

ANOTHER DAY, ANOTHER HUMILIATION

I knew it was going to be a bad day from the moment I leaned back in my chair while having breakfast, and fell clean through the kitchen wall. Most of me ended up in the dining room, except for my left leg which stayed in the kitchen. Mum wasn't happy. She hates it when I go through walls – even though I keep telling her it's a total accident and I can't control it. I head off to school, and I'm zipping and zapping in and out of focus. Today is the first rehearsal day for the Year Seven School Ball and I've been dreading this moment for weeks. It's OK for normal freaks like you. What's your biggest fear at a dance rehearsal? Standing on a girl's toes? Having to dance with a kid with bad breath? Going left instead of right during the Evening Three Step?

My heart bleeds for you. Now welcome to my world . . .

I'm standing on the polished wooden floorboards of the school assembly hall. All of us boys are on one side and all of the girls are on the other. Any other day of the year, we all just get on with the job of surviving our schooldays, regardless of whether we're male or female. At dance rehearsal, the school manages to make us feel awkward about who we are and forces us to look at our classmates as somebody we might have to consider romance with. Thanks a lot, Northcote High.

Actually, now I think of it, I'm the one thirteen year old who doesn't have that particular problem – wondering if romance is an option with one of my female classmates. What are the odds, do you think?

I can barely bring myself to do it, but I sneak a glance at the glory that is Ali Fraudulent, kind of looking from under the long fringe of my hair. If the girls in my year have an ultimate freak contender, then she'd be it, but I ache with the unfairness of it. Because Ali Fraudulent is a total babe. She's beautiful, tall, athletic, has pure white hair – which is admittedly weird at thirteen years old – and never ever speaks. To anybody. Not even to the teacher. She simply turns up each day, sits near the back of the class, apparently takes in everything that is being said, and then leaves. She can write OK, when she has to deliver an essay or something, but no sound has passed her lips. Even when somebody cracks a joke and she smiles, I've never heard her laugh.

But this is where life is so unfair. Whereas Ali is Queen Freak and gorgeous, I'm King Freak and a total dweeb. More or less average height but skinny to go with it, plus over-long hair and a slightly high-pitched voice. Oh yeah, and completely blurry. Long live the King.

And now, to prove that the Gods of Humiliation just don't know when to quit, Mrs Strangefloosie, the dance teacher, is bringing the boys and girls together to practise the tango and yes, to my horror and secret joy, Ali Fraudulent and I find ourselves herded together. I see her eyes briefly panic as she realises that Mrs Strangefloosie is blocking any avenue of escape, and I can't slip sideways either, because already Boris Scumm, our year's self-appointed bully and half a metre taller than me although only three months older, is right there, hissing, 'How perfect. The Freaks get to dance.'

'Leave us alone, Scumm,' I squeak, managing to take my eyes off Ali's mortified face to give him a glare.

Scumm leans in close and I'm almost overpowered by his body odour. 'I'm sure you two will have a terrific conversation,' he says, leering nastily at Ali, 'although babe, I don't know what you see in him.'

Scumm laughs like an idiot. A few of his henchmen join in. Ali and I are left, miserably looking at one another and not knowing where to begin. Then she puts out her right hand, slightly to the side, and raises her left elbow revealing her hip, and I momentarily forget all about Boris Scumm because you know what, she's inviting me to take my dancing position, and that means I'm about to hold Ali Fraudulent in my arms, a secret dream for at least the last year, and I don't have to let go for the duration of a tango.

I smile and lean forward and lean a little too far . . . and then I'm confused because I'm lying on my face and all

I can hear is laughter. Explosive laughter that threatens to take the roof clean off the school hall.

I lift myself up on my elbows and look back over my shoulder. When I see Ali's now horrified face looking back at me, I realise what has happened. I got so caught up in the moment that I fell clean through Ali Fraudulent.

Of course, that realisation means I go in and out of visibility like you wouldn't believe and end up so embarrassed and upset that if you were to look at me, I'd be little more than a cloud.

The only thing left is to get the hell out of there. As the cloud that is me stumbles past Ali, looking for the door, I manage to say above the laughter, 'I'm sorry.'

Ali opens her mouth, and I'm scared that she is going to laugh, that she will join the others with their cruel eyes and their savage fun at my expense. But she doesn't laugh. She closes her mouth again and just looks sad.

MEDICAL REPORT
ROYAL MELBOURNE HOSPITAL
FILE STARTED: DECEMBER 1994
UPDATED: JANUARY 2008
DR H. LONGABAUGH

PATIENT NAME: Hazy Retina (Hereby referred to as the 'Subject')
AGE AT MOST RECENT UPDATE (2008): 13 years old
PARENTS: Harold & Iris Retina, Fairfield
PATIENT CONDITION: Born 'out of focus'. An unusual physical condition, to say the least.

DESCRIPTION OF SYMPTOMS: Subject appears blurry around the edges and the features of his face are indistinct. To look at the Subject is to feel that you are looking through binoculars that are out of focus, or eyeglasses with the wrong prescription.

When Subject is very nervous, scared or uncertain, which is often (*see Psychological Report*), Subject can almost disappear, as though his entire body has become molecularly unstable. Subject has no control over this 'condition'.

Subject's parents report many occasions where Subject has fallen through walls, or been similarly physically 'unstable'.

Examples:
1999: At kindergarten, Subject reportedly 'lost' focus and accidentally walked *through* a see-saw. Vivid recall of, quote: 'other children screaming as I stood there, apparently impaled on the wood, wondering what the fuss was about.'
2005: At 10 years old, Subject recalls being accused by his cousin, Lucy, of cheating at hide and seek by making himself invisible. After much coaxing by counsellor, revealed that his other cousin, Olivia, had kissed him and he had involuntarily disappeared. Was mortified to be accused of cheating, and reports he could not deliberately make himself vanish.

2006: Ill-fated attempt at a family portrait, where photographer was unable to make Subject appear 'in focus'. Subject reports feelings of intense humiliation and shame.

PSYCHOLOGICAL EFFECTS: See full report, but Subject often refers to self as 'a freak'. Parents (Harold and Iris) report that he spends many hours in his room, reading comic books and refusing to go outside. Reports of loneliness at school. No friends.

HISTORY: A documented family condition.

According to Harold Retina (father), Subject is the third known member of Retina family to have said condition.

The first reported example apparently was an uncle in Perth, a son to Harold's father's brother. Not much known - he was 'kept out of sight' on a family farm in remote Western Australia.

Second known example: 'Uncle Blinky', the son of Harold's cousin, Gina, born in Sydney. Apparently born with his whole face pixelated, as though digitally distorted into small squares. Embraced condition and gained steady employment at TV stations, filling in for people being tried in the courts, whose faces must be obscured as they come and go from the Sydney Courthouse. Saved a fortune in special effects costs. Now believed to be overseas, living in New York where there is an entire TV channel devoted to court cases.

No known contact with Melbourne branch of the Retina family.

CHAPTER 2

HOME IS WHERE THE HURT IS

*T*he dance rehearsal was three days ago and I haven't left my room since, except to go to the bathroom, and to scavenge some food when my parents are at work or in bed so I don't have to talk to them.

About every hour or so, Mum comes and knocks on my door and asks if I'm all right. And I lie and tell her, yeah, I'm fine, but I want to be alone. I tell her I'm in the middle of a particularly great comic, one where the Southern Cross, an Australian Hero, is taking on an army of what look like alien vacuum cleaners.

All of which is true except for the bit about me being fine.

My mum thinks I need help. Not for the condition. What could anybody do? She says I need to see a counsellor. She says I need to learn to be more comfortable within myself. Hah! How could she know what it's like to be inside what is laughingly called my body, on the occasions my body is actually visible? Dad's even worse. Here's a typical encounter:

SCENE:

TONIGHT AT DINNER. HAZY RETINA IS RELATIVELY STABLE, MORE IN FOCUS THAN OUT, HAVING A RARE MOMENT OF NOT ACTUALLY THINKING ABOUT HIS FREAKINESS.

DAD: Say, Hazy, I've been meaning to tell you . . . did you read about that horse in China that was born with two heads? Apparently they managed to remove one of the heads so it's now more or less a normal horse, although I guess its neck would probably be left at a strange angle.

HAZY stares at DAD, trying to work out which of the nine separate incredibly painful torture techniques he's so far thought of will hurt him the most.

DAD: Still, I guess that nag won't be winning the Melbourne Cup any time soon, huh?

Cue animation sequence of kebab skewer through the eyeball. That would hurt the most. Even more than electric shocks to his groin . . . although, actually, now Hazy thinks about it . . .

MUM: *(worried, glancing at HAZY's blurred but murderous face):* Harold . . . let's talk about something else, dear.

DAD: I just thought the boy might find that interesting.

HAZY slams down his fork.

HAZY: Why? Because it is yet another story of how there are freaky things in the world that maybe, on a good day, might be even freakier than your absolute freak of a son, Dad?

DAD: Oh, err . . . I only said it because I know you like horses, Hazy.

HAZY: I hate horses.

Scene ends in icy silence.

You think I'm being mean and rotten to my old man, but trust me, when you've had to sit through this same conversation 100 or 200 times, with ever more freaky, disgusting subjects for him to compare with me, you'd be contemplating skewers to the eyeballs as well.

I go to reach for another comic but instead grab a book that my father bought me in yet another misguided attempt to make me feel good about my 'condition'. The book is called *I'm OK – You're OK* and was written years ago by some doctor, Thomas Harris. I can barely make heads or tails of it, apart from the fact that when we interact with other people, there are only four possible situations:

I'm not OK. You're OK.
I'm not OK. You're not OK.
I'm OK. You're not OK.
I'm OK. You're OK.

Options one and two pretty much cover my entire world, but that helps me how?

The book completely fails to mention freak-show children born out of focus, as far as I can tell, and once you rule out 'I'm OK' under any scenario, how was old Dr Harris looking?

I sigh, drop the book and pick up another comic until eventually Mum launches another sneaky bedroom raid and drags me out for dinner with her and Dad.

CHAPTER 3

CARROT TACOS FOR TABLE 47

I should have spotted something was up from the moment she said we were going to The Vegie Bar. Halfway along Brunswick Street, Fitzroy – the coolest street in Melbourne – it's a restaurant that would normally be way too fashionable for the Retina family to consider visiting, but it's become our regular place to eat out. The reasons are simple. One, it is the only place we know of that serves carrot tacos, much loved by my dad as some kind of aftershock remedy to his son carrying the family visibility curse. Two, nobody looks sideways at somebody who is not actually in focus. The locals are either too cool to do a double-take, or they find somebody being out of focus pretty routine. Tonight we're at our favourite table, down the back, near the corridor leading to the toilets.

'Did you have a go at reading that book I got you, Hazy?' says Dad.

'Dad, I tried. I really did. But what I need is a book entitled, *You're Not OK, You're Not OK*. Or maybe just *Freak*.'

'You are not a freak, Hazy Retina!' Mum weighs in. 'I've told you a million times how much I hate that word. You're just you.'

'Oh boy,' I say.

Dad says a little too loudly, 'Guess what!'

'What?' I reply. Mum looks worried.

'The way I hear it, if you had a microscope and magnified every centimetre of a person's skin, you'd find millions of tiny, too-small-to-see organisms living there.'

'Harold, dear –' says Mum.

'Totally crazy-looking creatures too, with tentacles and scales and lots of legs, eating dead cells to survive.'

I can't keep the edge out of my voice. 'This story had better not end with how I'm not as strange as I think, Dad.'

Dad looks uncomfortable. 'All I'm saying is, umm, well, isn't that pretty incredible. Gee, I wonder when we're going to get served?'

He is saved by the arrival of Lurch, my favourite waiter. I call him 'Lurch' after the servant in the Addams Family because he's got the same tall, gaunt, lumbering look. Lurch walks with a slowness that is completely at odds with The Vegie Bar's frantic kitchen and the other waiters and waitresses who hustle from table to table, delivering burritos, organic vegetarian pizzas and café lattes. He always seems to be on the verge of an important thought, but never quite seems to get there, instead frowning to himself and occasionally staring into the distance. It's as though Lurch is always holding himself back, somewhere deep inside. When he does talk, he rarely says more than one word at a time. And never looks sideways at my blur.

'Ready?' Lurch asks.

'Yes, we are,' says my dad, frowning at the menu one last time. 'Can we order two serves of carrot tacos, please?'

Lurch stares at Dad for what feels like a full minute, eyebrows raised.

'Fine,' he finally says, scribbling on his notepad. 'And?'

'I'll have pizza number seven, please,' says Mum. 'And a glass of the house wine.'

Number seven is a simple cheese and tomato pizza, known as a Margharita. Our family doesn't have the most expansive tastes when it comes to eating.

'And a cola,' I say.

'Sure,' Lurch says, with one last scrawl. Then he looks very thoughtful, gazes at me for a long moment, and drifts off, possibly to eventually place the order.

'Boy, he creeps me out,' my mother says.

'I like him. How do you think he got to be so tall?'

'Ate all his carrots when he was young,' says my father automatically.

'Yeah, that really helped me.'

Dad is about to launch into some kind of lecture about attitude, I can tell, but suddenly Lurch is back, having somehow silently drifted quite swiftly to our table. He is holding Mum's glass of wine and my cola. As he places them on the table with a long-fingered hand at the end of a long, long arm, I look up and find him staring at me.

'Gizmo,' he says. He's studying my T-shirt, which features a picture of Gizmo, a Hero said to have a thousand gadgets ready for use in any situation. 'Faker.'

'You don't believe in Gizmo?' I ask. 'Why not?'

Lurch looks at me for a long time. 'No evidence.'

This is the longest speech I have ever heard from Lurch.

'Superheroes have to work in secrecy. They deliberately don't let themselves have their photo taken.'

'That's rubbish, Hazy,' Dad snorts. 'How many times do we have to go through this? You're saying that with the thousands of video cameras and other surveillance devices available in the world, superheroes have never been caught by one of them, even on the edge of the frame?'

I know it sounds crazy, but Dad doesn't understand that I can't *not* believe in Heroes. 'What about the out-of-control satellite that was headed for New York recently? What made it explode as it entered the Earth's atmosphere?'

'The US military must have fired a rocket or something.' Dad shrugs.

'What if it was IncredoMan, ploughing to the heart of the satellite to blow it up?'

Everybody thought about this.

'Crap,' says Lurch.

'What about the avalanche that was all set to swallow Zurich? What melted it at the last second if it wasn't HotBabe?'

'Evaporation,' Dad sniffs.

'Global warming,' Mum suggests.

'Sunspot,' says Lurch.

'Fine! If you don't want to believe, you won't believe,' I say.

'Don't get upset, dear. You're starting to fade,' Mum says.

'All we're saying is that there's no photographic evidence of any superheroes,' Dad adds. 'You can't deny that.'

'Maybe they put some kind of invisibility bubble around themselves when they're working,' I say, but even as I say it, I know it sounds far-fetched.

Lurch gives me one last long look. 'Lucky guess,' he says, and drifts slowly away.

CHAPTER 4

THE VICTORIAN SOCIETY FOR THE BLURRED

*W*e head back to our car, but here's where Mum and Dad pull a massive swifty on me. Full of carrot tacos and soft drink, I fall into the back seat of the car and take a few moments to realise we're not travelling the usual streets towards our place.

'Where are we going?'

Mum and Dad are silent in the front seats. Dad turns the radio on and some old crooner's voice fills the car.

'Dad? Mum? Where are we going?'

Finally Mum turns to say, 'We're going to see somebody, dear.'

'Who?' I want to know. 'Friends?'

'Hopefully they'll be friends. They're certainly good people for you to know.'

Now I'm worried. What does that mean? I don't have

to wait long because soon we're in North Fitzroy and Dad flicks the left-hand indicator, turning out of St Georges Road into a side street. He finds a park and we all get out. And now I see it.

I briefly consider running, just running, but my brain is having trouble processing everything and I move like a robot beside my parents.

'The Victorian Society for the Blurred,' I read aloud from the sign above the entrance of the big red brick building on the corner. It looks like a converted church. Mum and Dad climb the steps and open the door.

'C'mon, son,' says Dad with a surprisingly gentle voice. 'We only want you to hear what they've got to say. What have you got to lose?'

My sanity, I think but don't say.

Inside the door is a massive hall designed for the days when people actually met to talk about things or gather in groups, for reasons that were not sport-related. Before TV, the internet and games consoles, in other words. A circle of chairs in the centre of the room is filled with some of the strangest-looking people I've ever seen. A lady with a clipboard stands, welcomes us and offers me a chair to her right. Mum and Dad sit somewhere out of sight, at the back of the hall.

LIST OF ATTENDEES
VICTORIAN SOCIETY FOR THE BLURRED
9 APRIL, 8 PM
(Notes by Counsellor Lillian Poindexter)

HUMPHREY SEPIA
Age: 60.
Condition: entire body is in black & white, as though on an old TV, pre-colour.

DORIS VERTIHOLD
Age: 52
Condition: A visual wave of her face and body moves up and down her shape, on a sort of loop.

BORIS DISTORT
Age: 28
Condition: Entire body is static, buzzing and hard to see.
(Would an antenna on his head improve his 'tuning'?)

(19)

STEVEN J. FLY
Age: 36
Condition: Face is divided into four segments with slightly different angles of his face in each section, like a console game in 4P mode.

JENNIFER SYNCHOFF
Age: 15
Condition: Mouth is on 'time delay' so you can see her lips moving a few seconds before the sound comes out.

JUSTIN BRYL
Age: 25
Condition: Smudged hair. Otherwise normal.
(Apart from school taunting, is this really a problem?)

MORGAN DEEJAY
Age: 13
Condition: Talks entirely in radio announcer clichés as though he's a 24-hour radio station on legs. No visual affliction.
(Possibility of employment delivering traffic reports during peak hour?)

TROY MURDOCH-QUIMBY
Age: 31
Condition: Has re-runs of animated program *The Simpsons* happening in a virtual screen on his forehead.

HAZY RETINA
Age: 13
Condition: Entirely out of focus. Seems to gain or lose visibility depending on mood and nerves.
(NEW MEMBER. Hostile and defensive on arrival – very out of whack visually. Was he born like this or is it some radioactive freak accident thing (again)?)

I'm checking out the woman who is clearly the counsellor in charge of this meeting for the Blurred. She is a small woman with white hair, hunched over in her plastic chair and clenching her hands together as though they are conducting some kind of independent wrestling match. They only stop when she writes notes on a clipboard. She's been going around the circle, asking questions of each person: How they are feeling? Are they are embracing their unique appearance? Does their family embrace them? Do they consider themselves empowered by their 'specialness'? Stuff like that. I've got her pegged as a flake already.

The bad news is that she is now grilling the kid next to me, so that means I'm up next. He has his hand constantly up to his right ear, as though he is wearing headphones, and can apparently only speak in radio clichés.

It's kind of hard to listen to him, so I watch the guy opposite me who seems to have a re-run of *The Simpsons* happening on his forehead. I watch for a while and realise I've seen it – the one where Bart and Lisa go to Duff Gardens.

Then I hear the kid next to me say, 'It's twenty-three past the hour and we'll be back with this blurry freak next to me right after this break.'

'Morgan, that's not very supportive,' says the counsellor.

'We apologise for that break in tasteful programming and invite you to enjoy the delightful sounds of this kid, whoever he is,' says Morgan.

I give him a glare but I'm losing focus so fast that he probably doesn't see it. I can feel everybody's eyes on me, and worry that I'm about to become invisible. Then again, that might mean I could sneak out.

'So, Mr Retina,' says the counsellor brightly, as though me fading into a mist is totally normal. 'Why don't you fill us in on why you're here?'

'Um, because my parents brought me.'

'And why do you think they might have brought you here?' She didn't miss a beat.

'Like, derr. I'm out of focus.'

'Is that a problem for you?'

I get such a surprise that I can feel myself snap in and out of focus a few times before settling somewhere on the wrong side of very blurry. 'Hello, Earth to Counsellor Woman? What do you think?'

Her smile doesn't waver. 'It doesn't matter what I think, Hazy. It's what you think. Would you prefer that your parents hadn't brought you to us tonight?'

'No offence,' I say.

'None taken. In fact, I'm very happy that you don't feel a need to be here. You obviously feel that your life is as great as it can be. That's fantastic!'

Of course, it's a trap, but I don't see it in time.

'I didn't say that,' I mumble.

'Excuse me, dear? I didn't quite hear that.'

'I didn't say my life is as great as it can be.' My visibility waxes and wanes again as I get worked up. 'My life sucks. People can barely see me, I get even worse when I'm scared or nervous or something, and all the kids at school call me Freak or Retard. One particularly nasty piece of work calls me "Fuzzy-Wuzzy Freak Show". My life is not good.'

'How do you feel when they call you names?'

'How do I feel? I hate it! But then again, you know what? They're right. I am a freak. I am a fuzzy-wuzzy freak show, even. I'm a retard. I'm challenged. I'm not all there.'

It comes pouring out of me and I'm surprised to find that I'm standing and shaking. I know that I'm all but invisible.

The silence after my outburst is only broken by Radio DJ boy saying quietly: 'All new music all the time. And now let's go down to the waterline with Dire Straits.'

'Morgan, please.' The counsellor's hands have finally stopped wrestling long enough for her to stroke her chin. 'Hazy, maybe it could be helpful if you stopped thinking of yourself in those terms. What if you start to think that instead of being "challenged", you're actually "special"? Has it occurred to you that you actually have some very special gifts?'

'Special because I fall through walls when I'm embarrassed?'

'Special because you have great qualities and a truly unique appearance. I know there are times I wish I could be invisible, like when my kids are fighting and they want me to make them dinner and I'm tired, for example. I think you're very special.'

Something, the ghost of an idea, sparks in my brain, but I can't quite grasp it. '. . . Special?'

'Very special.' Her hands are grappling again.

'Do you mean "special" as in "super"?'

'Super? Well, sure.' She looks uncertain. 'You're a special boy, and a super boy.'

I'm barely able to breathe. 'You mean I might be special like a superhero?'

The counsellor frowns. 'Well, that's not exactly what I meant but OK, if that makes you feel better about how you see yourself, sure. Maybe you do have a special "superpower".'

Her hands stop wrestling to put the quotation marks in the air.

'Now you can face the world, feeling proud, instead of embarrassed.'

'Super,' I whisper, hearing the word on my tongue. 'How has it never occurred to me that I'm super? That my condition is a superpower? How did I not realise?'

I'm standing again, and shaking, but in a whole new way. I feel like I could even kiss Morgan.

'Well, umm, we've certainly made some progress tonight,' says the counsellor, nodding enthusiastically to the rest of the group.

'I'm super,' I say. 'I'm super.' I say it again, and again. Then I can't help myself. I raise both fists to the sky and yell to the timber cathedral ceiling, 'I AM A HERO!'

The air feels fresh and new in my super-lungs.

And then I'm aware of the whole group staring at me.

'Umm, let's break for coffee,' suggests the counsellor.

CHAPTER 5

THE DARK BEFORE THE DAWN

*T*he ride home is tense.

'I have never been so embarrassed! What were you thinking, Hazy? Pretending you were a superhero in front of all those poor people.'

'But, Mum –'

'That was right up there with the first time my cousin, Blinky, went on television as an all-time moment in Retina humiliation,' Dad fumes.

'Dad, I –'

'We said we would go to the Vegie Bar on the assumption that you would fulfil your part of the bargain, young man.'

'What bargain?'

'Why don't you just go on that new "Australia's Craziest People" TV show and totally embarrass yourself and the family?' Dad says.

'Keep your hands on the steering wheel, love,' Mum says. 'But your father is right, Hazy.'

Now I'm getting mad. 'But Dad, you're the one always telling me people are much worse off than I am, that the condition is nothing to be ashamed of.'

'That doesn't mean pretending you're a superhero! All I've been saying is you're lucky you weren't born with three heads.'

What do you say to that?

Totally miserable, I watch the suburbs roll past my window.

It never occurs to me to look out the back windscreen and up. If I had, I might have noticed the shadowy figure flying along behind our car.

CHAPTER 6
LEON

Back home, I retreat to the safe haven of my bedroom, staring at the face of my all-time favourite superhero, Golden Boy. Actually, I'm looking at criminal genius the Boatman, reflected in Golden Boy's golden eye mask. Released by a leading newspaper as a souvenir of Golden Boy's memorable victory over the Boatman, when he saved Melbourne's Port Phillip Bay from a giant plug-hole three years ago, the poster is huge – two metres by one metre – and has long held pride of place on my wall. That movie had been huge. I love Golden Boy.

I ask the poster, 'What do I do with my life, Goldy?' But Goldy is silent. Maybe the disaster that is my life is too big a challenge even for the greatest of Heroes.

Mind you, he isn't exactly alone in his lack of ideas. I look around my bedroom, and dozens of the world's best

Heroes are equally mute on how I can turn my miserable life around. Apart from one or two patches of actual paint, my bedroom's walls are completely covered in posters, artwork, comic covers and other images of Heroes. I've got a large-format poster of the Ace next to my bed that cost me more than a month's pocket-money on eBay, but it's a beauty, with the Ace flicking giant playing cards at a faceless villain. The Southern Cross is up there too, posing with the medal he won as the southern hemisphere's top Hero for the year before. To his left, I have a poster of central Australia's most famous Hero, Big Red Rock, wrestling a nameless alien monster. The Rock's massive muscles are bulging in his desert-sand red bodysuit a moment before he lands a powerful right hook on the twelve-legged, four-headed, long-fanged creature from the planet Aaarngarn. The Flaming Torch is on the opposite wall, body flaming dramatically as he soars into the sky.

Nothing else can carry me away from the rotten mess that is my blurry life like these Heroes can. For a while, my walls had a couple of Jedis and boy wizards, but I always found myself covering them up with new images of masks, capes, bright uniforms and superpowers. If I was going to be honest, I might admit a guilty truth: that I tend to be pinning up more and more pictures of female heroes, and not just because I admire their superpowers. The inky purple curves of the Vampress; the blonde hair and fishnet stockings of the Black Sparrow; the positively indecent costume of Princess Hussy. I'm starting to find them every bit as interesting as QuasarMan's ability to fire a supersonic sound pulse at his enemies, or the Tiger's capacity for transforming himself into a, umm, tiger.

But no Hero, male or female, can dislodge Golden Boy as my favourite. Golden Boy can do anything, can beat anyone. One day, he'll be in the right place at the right time, and he'll get his chance to save the world. You watch. It's straight bad luck that he hasn't done it five times already. He's super-strong. He can fly like an eagle or a missile, depending on the need. He is smart and funny and clever and brave. I know all this because I have seen all the movies and read all his comics, many times. And he's a local – born and bred in Melbourne, my city.

I flick on the television, a recent addition to my room after much saving of pocket money, kindly matched dollar-for-dollar by my mum. I settle on a news bulletin where a big-jawed, boofy-haired newsreader is saying, 'Later, we'll be taking a special look at the always unique artwork of Melbourne's very own William Weld.'

The screen changes to show a massive twisted frame of iron, somehow fused together so that it looks like a crashed satellite.

'He's been creating this unique art for more than four decades, yet nobody in the art world has a clue how he does it.'

A breaking news story catches my interest. A streak of gold has been spotted, high over Brisbane, the capital of Queensland. Could it be Golden Boy? Nobody can say, and clearly the reporter doesn't believe it for a second. The truth is that for all the comic books, TV shows and websites devoted to Heroes, very few people can claim to have seen them in action, or to have solid evidence that they exist beyond the vivid imaginations of teenagers like me.

In fact, as far as I know, nobody has any evidence.

The Southern Cross's medal for Hero of the southern hemisphere, in 2005? Voted for by Hero fans at Hero Expo 05 at the Sydney Exhibition Buildings, and handed to a muscle-bound guy in a costume who my dad took great delight in proclaiming, loudly and with authority, was a former actor from the soap opera *Here and There*.

I prefer to believe, evidence or not.

Even now, when a Government scientist confirms that the golden streak was almost certainly a lost weather balloon, I'm prepared to trust my faith. It was him.

The newsreader comes back onto the screen. 'But first, an update on our headline story. Ashia?'

A blonde female reporter smiles at the camera, then assumes a serious face as the camera pans back to reveal another tangle of metal behind her. It might be a William Weld artwork, but in fact turns out to be a mangled white courier van.

'A bank robbery appears to have come to a bizarre end in the gold-mining town of Kalgoorlie after the thieves were found unconscious in their van, along with the missing payload,' the reporter says.

The screen switches to vision from the crime scene.

'Police are at a loss to explain a massive hole in the side of the van. It appears from tyre marks on the road that the van was stopped in its tracks while travelling at close to eighty kilometres per hour, and was then attacked from the side. The robbers are behind bars tonight, but are believed to be in shock, so police have been unable to interview them.'

The report has my full attention now.

'Rock,' I whisper.

'Yes, of course it's Rock,' says the large poster of the Southern Cross, next to the window.

I open my mouth to speak but my brain kind of lurches and I can only stare.

'That's the problem with Rock,' says the poster. 'He just doesn't get subtlety. Do you know what "subtlety" is, Hazy?'

'Erk,' I finally manage.

'It means doing something quietly and carefully so that nobody takes much notice, yet the effect is the same.'

By this stage, I can make out that it isn't actually the poster of the Southern Cross speaking, but a man who is blended entirely into the wall so as to be practically invisible.

'Who . . .?'

'Rock. Who else are we talking about? His idea of subtlety? To stand in front of a speeding van and then punch a hole in the side of it. Not exactly designed to slip under the media radar, that one.'

'No. Who? You?'

'Oh, sorry. I'm Leon, short for Chameleon. Call me Camel and you're in trouble, got it?'

The figure rises effortlessly and becomes bone-coloured, almost exactly matching the ceiling of my room. I don't miss the fact that the man, or creature or whatever it is, is flying.

Finally I manage a whole sentence. 'Heroes ARE real!'

Leon chuckles and lands lightly on the end of my bed, crouched in a ball, balanced on his toes and staring intently at me. 'Of course we're real, Hazy. You've known that all along. You just couldn't bring yourself to completely believe. It takes a while.'

'Why are you here?'

'Because you called for me. Unless I'm mistaken it was you, Hazy, who yelled earlier this evening, "I am a Hero"! Forgive me if I over-reacted, but we at the AFHT tend to take such a screech at face value, so I thought I'd come and say hello.'

'The AHFT?'

'No, the AFHT – the Australian Federation of Hero Types. It's the governing body for local Heroes, although it tends to play more of a management and administration role than actual governing. Most of the local Heroes know the rules and look after themselves. Except Rock, obviously.'

'How did you get in here?'

'Snuck through the front door alongside your mum and beat you up the stairs.'

'But I didn't see you at all.'

Leon sighs and looks at me as though he is regarding an infant. 'No,' he says very deliberately, 'you didn't. Because one of my superpowers is to be a chameleon and blend into backgrounds so I am, to all intents, invisible. Example: when you came into your bedroom and so did I . . . Are you planning on catching up any time soon, kid, or should I come back tomorrow?'

'I'm sorry, Leon, it's just a shock. So, you are here on behalf of the AFHT?'

'Finally, his brain creaks into gear,' Leon says.

'And you're here because I yelled out that I thought I was a Hero?'

'Not think, Hazy. You are.'

Now I'm unable to speak again. Leon laughs. 'It's OK,

I understand you being speechless. I felt the same way when the Southern Cross told me the truth for the first time.'

'The Southern Cross?' I look at the poster.

'Yep. I was sixteen years old. Like you, I'd spent my entire life thinking I was a freak, although it took me a while to realise why people always seemed to look right through me. Then I realised what was happening to my physical body . . .' Leon waves a hand in front of my bedroom lamp, and watches the image of the lamp run across his skin. 'Of course, I was freaked out. I went into a real funk until it occurred to me that I was superpowered. And, boom, the next thing I know, the Southern Cross shows up, shakes my hand, congratulates me on my power and flies off again. I'm only a Level C Hero but I've never looked back.'

'I have so many questions, I don't even know where to start.'

'Try them one at a time. In fact, I'll get you going . . . The first question is: "Am I really a Hero?" Right?'

I nod dumbly.

'The answer is yes. Stop pining about what a weirdo you are and come at it from the other direction: how many other people do you know who can walk through walls? Nobody. So enjoy your amazing abilities and get confident, stupid.'

'Get confident, stupid?'

'Just a Hero joke, blur-boy. In fact, we've been watching you for a long time, and I can tell you right now that you're a Hero, Entry Level, Grade Two.'

'But if you guys have been watching me for ages, how come you're only visiting now? Why didn't you tell me I was a Hero before this?'

33

Leon smiles. 'Standard Hero procedure. Nobody is a Hero until they decide they are a Hero.'

'So when I yelled out that I was a Hero –'

'That's what we'd been waiting for. I was right there, in the room, blended into the ceiling, ready to follow you home and catch up for this little chat.'

'How did you know it would be tonight?'

Leon smiles again. 'See, you haven't got your head around it yet. Has it ever occurred to you that there are Heroes in this city who have the power to know things before they happen?'

I think about this. 'Wow,' I say at last.

'Yeah, you'll be saying "wow" a lot over the next few weeks. It's all good.' Leon suddenly produces a bag from behind his back, and I'm caught between wondering what is in it and wondering if the bag is a chameleon as well.

But Leon is busy, digging around and throwing objects onto my bed. 'Rightio. On the assumption that you accept that you are a Hero, that you now officially realise and embrace this fact and are prepared to pledge yourself to that path –'

Leon raises an eyebrow in my direction and I nod my head furiously. 'I do. I am.'

'– then I have here your Hero Starter Kit. An official Hero Card, declaring that you are an Entry Level Hero, and that therefore villains can only attack you with certain moves and weapons while you find your feet, again assuming you plan to use your powers for good instead of evil.'

'I do. I will,' I say again, nodding even more. With a rush

of blood, I stand and put my hand over my heart, saying: 'I, Hazy Retina, pledge solemnly . . .'

'Kid, relax,' says Leon. 'I was just checking. OK, I also have a registration form for when you come up with your Hero name.'

'My Hero name?'

'What? You think I was born Chameleon? That the Southern Cross hasn't got an alter ego? That Green Pantheress's mother put that on the birth certificate?'

'Oh, right. When do I choose a name?'

'You have ninety days. After that, you either forfeit your Hero rights or Gotham City chooses a name for you.'

'Gotham City? You mean, as in . . .'

'Yep, that Gotham. Where the big-wig Heroes hang out. Don't sweat it. No offence but, trust me, lower-level Heroes like you and me don't ever have much to do with that league.'

'What else do I get?' I think about pinching myself to check this is all real but I'm so blurry with excitement that there's no way I could grab my skin, even if I wanted to.

'You get a Hero Beginner's Guide handbook, with a very useful foreword by Mr Fabulous.'

'Who?'

Leon looks up in surprise. 'Mr Fabulous. Haven't you read your comics? He was one of the original Heroes, way back in the 1930s. He's an all-time Hall of Fame Hero Legend. One of the first Triple A Level Heroes. Getting old now though.' He digs through the bag. 'You get an instruction manual for how best to keep a secret identity, common responses to tricky questions from everyday non-Heroes, and you receive a username and password for the Hero Central website – the URL is www.herohints.com. There's a lot of good information on there to get you going.'

Leon moves to the window, gently opening it. 'I think we're done . . . Oh, one more thing.' He digs into the bag one more time and produces a golden remote control, tosses it to me and nods towards the TV. 'I think you might find a new cable channel is now available on that box, activated by that remote control – which is already programmed with recognition software so it can only be activated by you. Channel 78737.' Leon takes in all the posters and Hero stuff littering my bedroom walls. 'I think you're going to love it.'

Then he wanders over to the desk and picks up the self-help book Dad got for me. Leon chuckles, points at me and says: 'I'm OK! You're OK! Cute.'

'Channel 78737?' I say, frowning.

'Try SMS . . . you'll work it out.' Leon winks and climbs onto the windowsill. 'Hazy Retina, it's been a pleasure. Don't let all this melt your mind. Take a day or two to get your head around it, and then do some research before even trying to take Hero steps. You'll be fine. You've got strong potential, kid. I could see you getting to Level C, maybe even the lower Bs. Good luck.'

'Leon, thank you so much. I don't know what to say.'

Leon smiles as he prepares to fly. Then he looks back at me and puts his right fist over his heart. 'Say the Hero motto: "A Hero is a Hero."'

'A Hero is a Hero,' I say, exploring the sound of the words.

'Yep. No matter what.'

And then Leon is gone.

I stare at the window. I stare at the TV. I stare at the poster of the Southern Cross, and wonder if I'm imagining a slightly different smile on the Hero's face, a knowing smile, a welcoming grin. I think I'm getting carried away. It's a poster. Is it possible I'm finally going mad? That my brain is as scrambled as the molecules of my out-of-focus body? Did I just imagine the whole thing?

A superhero called Leon?

There is a knock on my door.

Gotham?

Another knock.

'Hazy, dear? Did I hear voices in your room?'

A Hero is a Hero. No matter what.

'It was just the TV, Mum.'

'It sounded like your voice though, and a man.'

I feel myself smiling as I realise this is a historic moment. My first-ever chance to tell a lie to protect my secret identity! I haven't even opened the Hero handbook, although I've read enough comics to know the right way to go about this sort of thing. But I can't help myself. I do the exact opposite.

'Actually, Mum, it was me. I was talking to a superhero called Leon who is a chameleon. He walked through the front door when you did, but he had blended into the wall so you couldn't actually see him. We were just discussing my Hero status and talking about superhero matters.'

There is silence from the other side of the door until Mum says, 'You're really pushing your luck, Hazy Retina. This pretending to be a superhero has to stop, right now!'

'Yes, Mum,' I call sweetly to the door. 'Goodnight and have pleasant dreams. I know I will.'

I stand in front of the mirror and actually enjoy watching my body appear and disappear.

'A Hero is a Hero,' I say. 'No matter what.'

AN INTRODUCTION TO BEING A HERO,
BY MR FABULOUS
TRIPLE A HERO STATUS, 1937 –
FOUNDATION HALL OF FAME HERO,
HERO OF THE YEAR 1941, '43, '47, '52, '56, '65, '71
SINGLE-HANDED WORLD SAVES: 34
HERO TEAM-UP WORLD SAVES: 147

Hello Hero Wannabes.

So, you're all puffed up with your new Hero status, huh?

I don't blame you. I remember the feeling, all those years ago, and it's a good one.

But here's what I've got to tell you young punks: There's a lot of work ahead. You think the big time Heroes, the Triple As, were born just like that? Well, OK, some were, but the others had to work at it. Had to put in the hard yards. Had to sweat and learn and fail and keep striving.

That's what is ahead of you, kid.

And here's one other thing I want to impress on you. It won't be your actual power that stamps what sort of Hero you are. Yeah, yeah, yeah, you're all impressed by whatever your superpower is. You can summon the wind, or fly, or beam a heat ray from your belly button, or whatever your party trick is. Well, whoopee doo.

'Hero' comes from within. Yes, it's about learning to control and use your powers, but mostly it's about your attitude, your ethics and your willingness to give. For your fellow man. Or creature.

We don't all save the world every day. Sometimes, the most Heroic thing you might attempt all week is to help some old person cross the road. Or to untangle a dog's lead. Is that the stuff of comic book legend? No, but to that person, or that dog, you're Heroic right then, when they needed you. What I'm saying is that it's the little things that define a true Hero, not just the flashy rescues or the timely fist to an alien monster's jaw. If it has a jaw.

Got all that? Probably not, but try to give it some thought between weights sessions at the gym, huh?

Most of all, you will only be a true Hero when you believe. In you. And remember, a Hero is a Hero. No matter what.

Mr Fabulous

HERO RECOGNITION: A DISCUSSION
BY A. HERO

There are people wandering around in every city and every country of the world who have superpowers, but most don't realise it or don't want to know. Powers come in many forms and strengths. One person might have superior vision to everybody around him but never think about it, other than to wonder why everyone is peering at something in the distance when he can see it, crystal clear. Someone else might be able to hear a conversation across a crowded room and never consider that nobody else in the room can do the same thing. A long time ago in Gotham City, it was decreed that nobody would be recognised as a Hero unless they first voluntarily came to the realisation that they were a Hero, and were therefore prepared to accept all that being a Hero means.

OFFICIAL RATINGS SYSTEM

Dateline: Agreed and enforced across the entire Hero and Villain world, as decided at the 1967 One-time Summit between leading bad guys and Heroes.

It is decreed that Heroes are to be rated, according to their abilities, actual powers and experience, from Entry Level, Grade Two through Level G, Level F and so on up to Triple A. Meanwhile, villains are rated by Categories, from Category 8 for the worst Super Villains down to Category 1 for lesser criminals such as, say, a shoplifter with two or more offences.

Heroes and criminals must declare their Level or Category before fighting. The following rules outline which weapons and powers that the more powerful person can use against an opponent who has a lesser rating, and therefore less ability. The superior being is allowed to fight as hard as they like, but within certain guidelines.

(that's me, folks)

(able to leap tall buildings, faster than a speeding bullet, much more powerful than a train ... you get the idea)

(Note to Heroes: Let's not forget the incident that led to the formation of these rules, which were agreed after an over-enthusiastic but immensely-powerful young Hero, Kid Laser, accidentally vaporised five teenagers who had been stealing garden gnomes in February 1965.)

SUBJECT: New Hero website introduction

Dear Mr Retina,

Congratulations on your confirmed status
as a Hero, Entry Level, Grade Two.

You are invited to visit our website,
www.herohints.com, for news, advice, tips
and other Hero-related matters.

We trust it will be of service to you.

Your username and password for the site are
as follows:

username: hazy_retina
password: carrot_taco

Yours in Heroism,
B. Canary,
International Hall of Heroes,
Gotham

CHAPTER 7

THE WORST WEDGIE IN HUMAN HISTORY

*T*hat was last night and now I'm back at school, finally dragged from my room after an unexpected room invasion by my mother, some air freshener and a stern talking-to about the value of a good education.

I can hardly walk I'm so tired, but I'm grinning from ear to ear. Scumm and his buddies hurl insults at me and I just breeze on by. I have no doubt that during the three days of my absence, the words 'freak', 'retard' and 'loser' have been dramatically downgraded in their usage among the crueller sections of the school population, and now that I'm back, normal taunting can be resumed. But today is a day I am untouchable and, for once, it's not because my body is more mist than skin and bone.

I might be Entry Level, Grade Two, the lowest level there is, but I'm a Hero.

Of course it was too good to last. Of course I shouldn't have come to school. Second class I find myself heading to maths and that means Ali will be there. Instantly I can feel myself becoming a cloud again and I try to think about IncredoMan's epic battle against the Fangstaaaaaaar Nine on the Planet Elginon, a comic I was reading last night. Distracted, my body takes shape again, as much as it will in a school environment, and I'm even more relieved, once I'm sitting, to realise that Ali has worked hard to get a desk on the other side of the room and won't meet my eye. Her ghost-white hair hangs down to cover her face like a wall, which suits me fine. Now I think about it, she wasn't about to say anything anyway, right? But I can feel the eyes and hear the sniggers as the rest of the class enjoys my struggle.

It's hard to believe but at recess, things get worse. I come around a corner and there's Boris Scumm, terrorising a kid – the tuckshop's brick wall expertly between him and any possibility of a teacher's line of sight. One thing for Boris, he's a natural bully. Big, dumb and street-smart.

The other kid is from my year level but we've never actually shared a class. I know his name, though. It's Frederick Fodder. He's a short, stocky kid who is known mostly among our year for his bizarre antics on the football field. Despite his lack of size, Fodder has a tendency to fly for big marks, climbing over the pack to catch the ball, only to suddenly shoot off in the wrong direction, landing heavily metres away from the action. It looks hilarious, no matter how many times you see it.

Usually Fodder hangs out with Simon Fondue, possibly the most shy and second-most quiet kid in Year Seven, always mumbling and playing with his fingers. When Fondue walks past, all you can hear are mumbles and clicks. I look around for him now and find him, hiding behind the tuckshop door, looking terrified.

Fodder, on the other hand and to his credit, looks more mad than scared, even with massive Scumm looming over him plus at least five henchmen lurking.

'What's the matter, *Nerderick*?' Scumm sneers. 'No footballs to completely miss?'

'You think I'm scared of you?' Fodder says. 'Why don't you and your five girlfriends leave me alone and go play house?'

Even Scumm blinks. Nobody speaks to him like that.

'Man, you are so dead, Nerderick.'

'Leave him alone, you big ape!' An even smaller girl, also stocky and with the same black hair as Frederick, appears behind Scumm, hands on hips in a defiant pose. 'Why don't you pick on someone your own size – like a refrigerator?'

Scumm turns slowly to look at her, which is a disaster for me because, yep, the girl happens to put me right in the bully's line of sight. Instantly, Fodder and the girl are forgotten.

'Hey, Fuzzy-Wuzzy Freak Show, is there something wrong with my eyes or are you being a freak, as usual?'

'Leave me alone, Scumm.' I can already feel myself wavering badly.

'I'd love to but you're such a freak I just can't take my eyes off you, Fuzzy-Wuzzy Freak Show. Oh actually, I can't keep my eyes on you.'

This is pretty much the extent of a Boris Scumm conversation.

'Just drop it, Scumm. I'm leaving.'

I am fast losing visibility and I try to get out of there, to run to the library and escape, but suddenly Scumm's massive hand is grabbing the elastic of my underpants. I get such a shock that I instantly lurch wildly out of focus, just as Scumm yanks, resulting in Scumm falling backwards, me falling forwards and both of us ending on the ground.

I am almost invisible with embarrassment and anger while Scumm has a strange, shocked smile on his face. I almost throw up when I see he is holding my underpants in his paw. I lost so much of my physical presence in the attack that Scumm has yanked my undies clean through what is left of my body. Cue mass schoolyard laughter.

Scumm sniggers. 'SpongeBob undies?'

Why had I ever left my room?

Later, holed up in the library with my head buried in a comic, both hands over my ears, trying uselessly to shut out the laughter and taunts still echoing, I become aware of a presence at my side. It is Frederick Fodder.

'Hazy?' he says.

'You know my name?'

He shrugs, almost apologetically. 'Everyone knows your name, Hazy.'

'Yeah, I guess they would,' I say. 'You're Frederick, right?'

'Champion of the football pinball.'

I find myself smiling. 'I liked how you stood up to that gorilla out there.'

'That's what I wanted to talk about,' he says. 'I'm really sorry it ended the way it did. It was my fight, not yours.'

'Scumm picks on anybody he thinks is vulnerable. His line of sight could just as easily have gone from me to you.'

'Well, anyway, I'm sorry.'

'Thanks,' I say, and I mean it, all the while thinking that this might be the longest conversation I've ever had with a fellow pupil. 'Who was the girl?'

Frederick rolls his eyes. 'My little sister. She told me that she'd mysteriously known that I was about to get into a fight, so she'd come to save me.'

'Wow. Is she that tuned in?'

'Not when it comes to remembering it's her turn to feed the dog.'

I laugh and so does Frederick. I'm certain I've never done that with anybody at Northcote High before. Just for a moment, I feel something that might be sunshine in my life.

It doesn't last. Scumm catches up with me again on the way home from school. Actually, I think Scumm himself is a little freaked out by the underwear incident so he leaves it to his chief assistant bully, a hulking fourteen year old known as Cam the Man, to try and rub my face in some dog poo that is conveniently lying on the footpath. Luckily I literally slip through Cam the Man's thick fingers moments before my face reaches the ground and his hand ends up in the poo. I run the rest of the way home, lungs screaming.

Some Hero.

CHAPTER 8
GETTING STARTED

For the next four nights, I do pretty much nothing but read the Beginner's Guide, surf herohints.com and watch Channel 78737, which turns out to be an entire TV channel dedicated to superheroes. It's like a 24-hour news station, but only addressing Hero matters and to a Hero-only audience.

No matter what time I click on, the channel is in full flight. The newsreader is either a muscly hero in a dark suit with a black cape (!) or a smart-looking blonde woman in a clinging lycra costume, wearing a small mask.

NEWSREADER: A lucky escape for Detroit Level B'er the Echo when Category Five super-villain, the Iron Bar, made an unexpected foray into the Motor City last night. The Echo was forced to fight his way past nine of the Iron Bar's henchmen before turning his sonic echo on the Villain himself. The Iron Bar was able to repel the audio with a shield of metal, but the Echo found an angle off a distant glass roof with which to rebound his vocal attack and smack Iron Bar from behind. The Villain is now (chuckle) behind bars, pun intended. Nice work, Echo.

In other news, Roman Hero the Gladiator has told HeroTV that the arrival of a strange Hero, calling himself Coliseum Magnifico, was more of a hindrance than a help in last night's narrow win over Death-Raccoon. The unknown Hero claimed to be a 'Bow', allegedly able to travel by rainbow, though international Hero authorities remain sceptical. And now to Hero Horoscopes . . .

(50) It's heaven. Sometimes HeroTV features small one-minute packages celebrating 'Great Moments in Heroics', with a recap of spectacular victories by Heroes over arch Villains, alien invaders or natural disasters.

What really surprises me is that I already know some of the stories. Super Surfer's classic battle against the SharkMen of Atlantis? Yeah, I'd read that one in MG Comics, Issue #473 (I looked it up to check). Star Princess's against-the-odds win over the Giant Alligator of the Planet Quaoar? Galactic Comics, Issue #729.

I'm astounded to discover that while ordinary people (including me, until a few days ago) think comics are merely fantasy cartoons for kids to read, they are actually the chosen newspapers of the Heroes themselves, a way of keeping in touch with each other's exploits. Kind of a paper-based Hero blog, or a way of providing a more detailed account of their adventures than a quick news grab on HeroTV. I go back to my boxes of old comics and devour them all over again, catching up on the exploits of the inhabitants of my new world.

The Beginner's Guide makes it clear that Heroes should not even think about presenting their new secret identity to the world until they have come up with an impressive, professional costume and a super name. Apparently, the Hero executive in Gotham doesn't want Heroes in any corner of the world wandering around in a bad tracksuit with an old towel as a cape. It's a matter of pride, as much as anything. To inspire fear and awe among those they battle, Heroes must look the part. Golden Boy is even pictured in the Guide, presented as a literally shining example, his costume catching sunlight as he strikes a dramatic midair pose, looking every inch a top-line Hero.

Coming up with my costume isn't easy. I finally have the idea while walking home from school at dusk, that beautiful silvery time of the day just before night falls. Catching sight of myself in a shop window, I realise that between the soft silver light and my usual blurriness, I am close to invisible. There and then, I decide on silver for my costume's primary colour. Even better, in Olympic medals silver is just behind gold, and I'm happy to leave the winner's medal to Golden Boy at this stage of my career.

Of course, I look ridiculous in my first attempt at a costume, which is your standard skin-tight lycra Hero outfit. Whoever decided that superheroes should wear bodysuits was clearly not thinking beyond the 1930s and 1940s, when carnivals and acrobats might have been more popular.

In the new millennium, there is no way to walk around in a silver figure-hugging costume and not feel like a goose, superpowered or not, especially when you're a gangly, thin, thirteen-year-old boy who's a long way from having the sort of musclebound chest that can fill out a costume like the Triple A Level Heroes.

I go back to the drawing board and almost throw out the whole silver idea, wondering if a white costume would show the dirt too much? Or would people think I was a cricketer? Or, worse, a lawn bowler!

But then I realise that silver isn't the problem: it's the design. I even log into www.herohints.com to confirm that there aren't many Heroes out there wearing silver or with silver in their name. There's only Silverman, SilverSon, Silvery Dilvery, Prince Silver, Captain Silver, Silver-King, Super Silvery, Soulsilver, Silverfish, Miss Silver, Mrs Silver, Son of Silver, Silvero, Silvery, Silver Steve, Silverous, Super Silver, Silverado, Silverman, Silvergirl, Siverboy, Silverperson, Silverspider, I-Can-Believe-It's-Not-Silver, Silveroo and Silvery Moon.

See, I've practically got the colour to myself.

The book also warns new Heroes not to make a hasty decision on their super name, as this will be their immortal signature. Harsh as it is, the Handbook even mentions 'Clarence the Really Terrific Robot Battler', a 1960s Hero, as a warning. Poor Clarence did some good work but could never be taken seriously. While I have ninety days to register a name, I'm advised to use that time to think carefully and come up with a good one.

At school the next day, all I can think about is potential names.

The Blur?
Blinky 2?
Nephew of Blinky?
Super Squint?
Eyestrain?
Captain Fuzzy?
Misty?
Misty Man?
The Mistmeister?
Misto?
Maybe not something to do with Mist.
Cloudy?
Blur Boy?
Blurrific?
Invisi-Man?

53

Sitting at my desk, I throw all of them out. I'm staring out the window, watching Simon Fondue walk past, deep in concentration. It must be a trick of the light or a reflection of the sun because something bright keeps flashing on Simon's hand but I can see his hands are empty. Weird.

Suddenly I become aware of my humanities teacher, Mrs Restroom, looming at my desk. 'Hazy Retina? What is it with you today? Can't you focus for just one minute? Is it that hard to focus on a blackboard? I'm not talking about – you know – *you*. I'm talking about your attention. What do I have to do to get you to focus?'

Mrs Restroom slams her fist on my desk.

'HAZY RETINA. ARE YOU FOCUSING?'

'Yes, ma'am, I'm focus. I mean, I'm focusing. This is science, right?'

Everybody laughs. I get a detention. I should be embarrassed, but I'm not. I'm too busy thinking about what just came out of my mouth, if accidentally.

'I'm Focus,' I said.

Job done. I've got a Hero name.

CHAPTER 9
CAR CRASH

*T*hat night, at 2 am, I'm standing shivering in a car park at the eastern end of the city centre, not far from Parliament House. From around the corner, maybe fifty metres away, a new-looking Ford sedan sails through the air on its side and slams into a concrete pillar, exploding the car and taking giant chunks out of the cement. The noise is terrifying.

Involuntarily I take three steps backwards and bump into Melbourne's Chief of Police, the miracle being that I'm solid enough to actually make contact.

I mumble an apology to the Chief, who raises an eyebrow at me, her arms folded across her chest. She sighs, looks at a man in a suit standing with her, and shakes her head.

I'm wearing jeans that are spray-painted silver, a silver T-shirt with a large 'F' emblazoned on it, Dunlop Volley runners, also spray-painted silver, and a silver cape. Oh, and a silver mask across my eyes. Sure, my costume doesn't quite match up to the self-sufficient yet protective living skin of Captain Alien, but I'm on a smaller Hero budget. The cape was essential. When I tried to imagine myself out there, facing genuine criminals, the dream always seemed to involve clutching a fistful of cape and throwing it around myself so that I disappeared like a magician into its folds and was gone. Capes are dramatic, look great and are very super. Nobody wears a cape around, apart from Heroes. For a new Hero like me, not even convinced I am a Hero, a cape can carry the bluff a long way. Plus, and this is not to be taken lightly, a really long, cover-all cape can hide the fact that the rest of my costume is basically crap.

Something the Chief of Police is probably thinking right now. We both flinch as a Volkswagon Beetle soars through the air and is totalled against the far wall of the car park.

The Chief asks, 'What was your name again?'

'Focus!' I say it proudly, chest puffed, although I'm now so blurry she probably can't tell.

'And your plan for beating Car Crash is . . .?'

'Just formulating it now, ma'am,' I say.

We look at each other and both know this is a total lie. I've got nothing.

'And what about them?' she says, jerking a thumb at three other Heroes a few metres away.

'You'd have to ask them, Chief. Um, I'll have a word if you like.'

She looks tired as she shakes her head. 'Tell you what, why don't we all just sit tight for a bit. No sense rushing in.

Are you by any chance new as a Hero?'

'Yes I am,' I admit.

'Grade D, maybe? Or a C?'

'Actually, I'm Entry Level, Grade Two.'

'Oh boy,' she says. 'Ohhh boy. As I was saying, let's not rush into anything.'

The reason I'm here is because I'm completely ignoring the advice of Leon and the Hero Beginner's Guide, which cautions against charging into the world and immediately attempting to battle the forces of evil or attempt daring rescues. It says a start-up Hero should not launch into actual Hero work straightaway, but should wait until he or she is comfortable with their range of powers and realistic about their abilities.

Stuff that. Having waited my whole life to be a Hero, I'm not waiting any more.

I sneak a glance around the corner but Car Crash is on the other side of the lifts. All I can see is his enormous hulking shadow on the wall as he crouches, picks up the shadow of what looks like a massive 4WD and hoists it over his head. I swing back to safety just in time to hear the metal splinter. A massive wheel bounces past our hiding spot.

Car Crash is the reason I'm here and not in bed. I saw a news flash on HeroTV an hour ago and snuck out of the house. Thrillingly for me, this monstrous ball of evil is redefining road rage by planning to destroy every vehicle in Melbourne, one car at a time. Part of me is wild with excitement to be here, loving the fact that the everyday population is sleeping peacefully, with no idea that a mid-level super-villain is on a rampage. Unless I can stop him.

Or the Victorian Government can pay him forty million dollars to hold off on his threat. These last few minutes, Car Crash has been getting antsy, wondering where the money is.

A BMW flies and dies. My ears ring from the noise. And I still don't have a plan.

I look again at the other Heroes present. Two youths are slumped against the wall, and a small Hero is bouncing up and down on the spot, smiling cheerfully at anybody who looks his way. I should go over and talk to them, see if they've got any good ideas, but I can already tell they won't.

The youths appear to be asleep for a start.

And then there is a golden light, glowing from the air above the lane outside the five-storey car park. My heart skips a beat. Can it be? I already know it is. I surge to complete invisibility with excitement and expectation as the light grows brighter, and then I watch him land, effortlessly stepping out of the sky.

A Holden ute smashes into the nearest wall but Golden Boy only glances at it, a small frown on his golden face, as though a mosquito had wafted past. Then he walks over to where we are standing.

'Golden Boy! Thank God!' says the Chief of Police.

'Officer,' Golden Boy nods. He looks at the man in the suit who is staring at him even more goggle-eyed than I am. Obviously, by his face, he hasn't seen many superheroes in action.

'Is security clear?' Golden Boy asks the Chief.

'It is.'

'Car Crash looks like he means business.'

'We got here about twenty minutes ago. He's thrown ten or twelve cars and he's not slowing down,' the Chief says.

'His personal record is forty cars, or thirty-two cars and two trucks, depending on which statistics you follow. It could be a long night.'

'How do you know all that? Have you battled him before?'

'No, but I Googled him on the Golden Computer Remote on my way here. Have you sealed off the area, Chief?'

'I have officers stopping traffic at both ends of Collins, Little Collins and Bourke Streets, as well as Spring Street and Exhibition. There's a perimeter, citing road works, a kilometre out in all directions.'

'Nice work.' Golden Boy swings around and looks at the nervous politician. 'Who are you? You're not the Premier.'

'Public relations,' says the large man, sweating heavily as he steps forward. 'Here to make sure the Government doesn't get blamed for damaged vehicles. Not that we'd dream of blaming you, of course, Golden Boy. Ha ha ha. It's nice to meet you, by the way. I never realised –'

'We work hard to make sure most people don't realise,' Golden Boy says. He looks hard at the man. 'I hope you will respect that and keep our confidence.'

'Of course.'

'Thank you. All right, I'm setting up a hero haze,' he says, pushing a button on his golden glove. A blur appears outside the car park in all directions. 'Incidentally, have you considered paying him the money?'

The PR man splutters. 'The forty million? Do you think the city is really in danger?'

Golden Boy somehow sparkles even though it is a dark night. 'It would be if I wasn't here, yes.'

The Chief of Police coughs. 'Actually, Golden Boy, there are some other Heroes here as well.'

Golden Boy hasn't even noticed us, standing off to the side of all this.

'There are? Who?'

'I'm, err, not familiar with them, if you get my drift.'

'Oh dear.'

'Yeah, exactly.'

Suddenly, from the other side of the car park, a deep voice yells, 'Where's my money?'

There is a whistling noise and a Landcruiser shatters into metal jigsaw pieces metres from Golden Boy's head.

'Stall him,' Golden Boy says.

'Stall him?' The Chief of Police takes off her hat and scratches her head. 'How?'

'I don't know. Tell him the ATM is broken.'

And now Golden Boy comes over to us, leaving the Chief and the PR guy behind. I find myself face to face with Golden Boy for the first time. My greatest Hero. I'm numb with happiness. This is a dream come true.

'OK, you little brat, listen up and listen good,' he says harshly. 'Stay out of my way or I'll hurt you more than Car Crash ever could. Got it?'

'Huh?' I say stupidly.

'What level are you, kid?'

My voice sounds squeaky. 'Entry Level, Grade Two.'

'Then you should be home, tucked up in bed with your teddy bear, not here getting in my way.'

I can't even speak.

'Nothing annoys me more than wannabe Heroes getting in the way of us real Heroes. You only make the job harder.'

He looks at me, so blurred now in surprise and shock that I'm more cloud than boy. 'Are you sure that isn't just a nasty skin condition?'

'Golden Boy, I've always thought you'd be . . .'

'Brilliant? Yeah, I am, which is why I don't want nappy-wearing try-hards like you cramping my style.'

With that, he turns to the other Heroes, and I'm left trying not to cry.

The two youths are still sitting together, slumped so that their heads are almost jammed between the wall and the ground. Golden Boy could be forgiven for wondering if they've been knocked out. The other figure waves wildly at him and jumps up and down as Golden Boy approaches.

Golden Boy crosses his arms. 'Evening, Heroes. Who are you lot then?'

The Hero who is standing rushes up to Golden Boy and enthusiastically shakes his hand. 'Hi there, Golden Boy. Great to meet you, I mean *really* great to meet you! I'm Prince Perky!'

Golden Boy looks at his own golden-gloved hand as though it might be contaminated. 'You have powers?'

'Oh yes, sir! I'm only a Level F Hero but boy, I think even that's fantastic. It must be terrific being a Level Triple A like you are, Golden Boy.' Prince Perky cocks his head and looks serious. 'Is your life just fabulous?'

Golden Boy sighs and turns to the two Heroes slumped

against the wall. They look at him with half-asleep eyes from under over-long fringes. Their uniforms are pure black but filthy with dirt, and one has a nose stud. They haven't moved since I got here.

Golden Boy says, 'And I'm dying to know who you two are.'

'Like, care factor zero about what you think, over-achiever. We're the Slacker Bros, dude.'

He pronounces 'bros' like you'd say 'goes'.

'You're Heroes?'

'Whatever,' says one.

The other sighs deeply. 'Yeah, like Level G means anything anyway.'

It's then I realise their slouched pose would be perfect for if you were leaning against a couch, instead of a car park wall. Their arms are bent at the elbow and their hands are unconsciously still in position to hold a Playstation or Xbox control.

'So were you guys planning to get up and sort out this super-villain any time soon?' Golden Boy asks.

One of the Slacker Bros shifts slightly, so he can scratch his butt. 'The car vandal guy?' He sniffs. 'Oh yeah . . . I guess . . . Eventually.'

'Yeah, we'll get to it,' says the other.

'When exactly?' asks Golden Boy.

'. . . Later.'

'I think everything is going to work out fine!' It's Prince Perky. 'I really think that between all of us we can do something really positive and really successful.'

'I have another idea,' Golden Boy says. 'You four losers

don't move, so you don't get hurt.'

I'm stung by the word 'losers'.

But Prince Perky is nodding so enthusiastically his head might fall off. 'That is a BRILLIANT plan!'

The Slacker Bros stare at the golden Hero.

'Whatever,' one finally manages.

I still can't speak, but Golden Boy doesn't care if I have anything to say anyway.

He steps out from behind our protective concrete wall and is greeted almost instantly by a flying Toyota sedan. He puts out a hand and stops it dead, and it crashes to the floor in front of him. Then he flies, actually flies, over it and I hear him say, 'Car Crash, I am officially declaring myself to be a Level Triple A Hero. What is your level?'

'Category 5, but that doesn't matter because we're not going to fight. They're going to pay.'

'Wrong and wrong,' says Golden Boy's voice.

I hear a sharp slap of skin on skin, and then silence. Golden Boy stalks back around the corner.

'Over to you, Chief,' he says, and presses a button on his golden glove. The haze around us vanishes. 'Hero haze lifted. We can all go home. Goodnight, gentlemen, Chief.'

'Thank you, Golden Boy! You saved the city,' yells the PR man.

'All part of the service. Remember, mum's the word.' He turns to us. 'As for you lot, get a real job.' He walks back out to the alley and then takes off, vertically, with a faint whoosh.

We all watch the golden Heroic light fade in his wake.

'That was just fantastic!' says Prince Perky.

'Like, yawn,' replies a Slacker.

63

I trudge home in my cheap costume. School starts in less than four hours. I really should try to sleep. I try to put Golden Boy's sneer out of my mind. But I can't.

HERO BEGINNER'S GUIDE
GETTING STARTED

So you charged off and tried to be a Hero.

Congratulations. You're now one of the approximately ninety-eight per cent of new Heroes who ignored our advice and charged out into the Hero world, without preparation or confidence. Of those ninety-eight per cent, maybe three or four Heroes each decade handle themselves well and arrive on the scene fully formed and ready for action. The chances are, if you're reading this, you're not one of them.

So we say again: hone your skills, build your confidence, confirm your costume and name. If your city has a 'Heroes Anonymous' meeting, go along and meet other Heroes. Work together on your skills. And next time, pay attention when we tell you that the road you're taking is no picnic.

UNFRIENDLY FELLOW HEROES

New arrival Heroes may be surprised to occasionally meet established Heroes who are not particularly welcoming, or are even openly hostile. Usually this betrays a lack of self-confidence on the part of the unfriendly Hero. Don't take such unexpected abuse personally. We can almost guarantee that the Hero being nasty has personal issues to work out, or a deep-seated insecurity that makes him or her feel threatened by new Heroes arriving on the scene. It's just like everyday bullies who pick on other kids to hide their own inadequacies. The reality, sadly, is that there is no shortage of crime for all of us to fight, and that there is a place in the Hero world for everybody, of every level of grading, power and personality.

CHAPTER 10

HEROES ANONYMOUS

The next night, I decide to go to Heroes Anonymous.
There's no doubt I have a lot to learn.

'You're out again, Hazy dear?' says Mum, looking
up from the TV.

'Warhammer painting night, Mum. In at Games
Workshop at Melbourne Central.'

'But dear, it's Saturday night. Are you sure you should
be wandering around in the city? Isn't it dangerous?'

'I shouldn't be late and the tram stop is right outside
Melbourne Central. I'll be fine.'

'Leave the boy alone, Iris,' says Dad, looking out from
behind the newspaper. 'It's nice he's making some friends,
even if they are nerds.'

'Warhammer people are not nerds.' I feel compelled
to stand up for my so-called friends, even though I made

the whole Warhammer thing up. I've read magazines and cruised through Games Workshop. I could get into it. 'Warhammer demands imagination and good skills at painting and other crafts.'

'Says you. At least you're likely to meet people even stranger than you – and I say that supportively,' he adds hastily. 'Did you know, Hazy, that there is a man in Kazakhstan who is reportedly able to remove all four fake limbs and roll the 100 metres in less than eleven seconds? That's almost Olympic time.'

'Hush, Harold,' says Mum. '*The Bill*'s about to start.'

Before long, I'm in a dark alley in the city centre, near the corner of Spencer and Lonsdale streets, standing outside the enormous brick wall of a disused power station.

For a moment, I laugh. I think about how the counsellor and regular visitors to the Victorian Society for the Blurred would react if they could see me now. Because I'm going to a whole different meeting.

The abandoned station has stood here for years, derelict and forgotten, reportedly riddled with hazardous asbestos, a dangerous hideout for the city's homeless and desperate.

Ironically, directly across Lonsdale Street is the headquarters of the *Age* newspaper, one of Melbourne's two big morning papers. Yet the dozens of reporters who work at the paper have never once spotted the variety of people in colourful, strange costumes descending on the power station every Wednesday evening.

According to the Melbourne blog of herohints.com, every now and then one of the wild-haired crazy homeless people who live illegally in the power station storms into the newspaper's foyer telling ridiculous stories of having seen somebody fly through the air. The newspaper reporters apparently roll their eyes, shake their heads sadly and send the crazy type back onto the street. Because in the rational, switched-on world of the journalists, Heroes don't actually exist. Remember?

Which shows what they know.

I'm standing in this creepy dark alley when I hear something overhead. It's hard to tell in the dark but I think I see a black dot lurch across the sky and smack into the giant chimney of the power plant. Whatever it is slides down behind the massive wall, falling out of sight. I'm probably imagining it but I even think I hear a distant groan.

I've been trying to get into the power station for more than twenty minutes. Of course, being loaded with dangerous radioactive chemicals and other hazards, and having been closed down more than fifteen years before, the power station is surrounded by high walls and wire fences with barbed wire.

Heroes Anonymous, a self-help branch of the Australian Federation of Hero Types aimed specifically at new heroes, works on the theory that if you can't even get into an abandoned building, you have no right to be there anyway. Herohints.com has told me where I need to be and when, but that doesn't help me get past the fence.

In the end, pure luck solves my problem. I walk even further down the sinister alley, trying to find some kind of crack in the thick brick wall, when there is a crash and, by the time I swing around to see that it is only a rat jumping out of a rubbish bin, I've received such a fright that my body blurs to the point of invisibility and I fall clean through the wall.

I straighten my silver cape (now with black backing), run a hand through my mess of hair, adjust my mask and make sure the F is straight and black against my silver T-shirt. I'm also now wearing silver-sprayed cargo pants. I figured so many pockets mean I won't need a bulky utility belt and Hero officials can't frown about the jeans thing. I'm still in silver-painted Dunlop Volley shoes, but hopefully nobody will notice. I want to look good for this meeting. I creep further into the power plant, looking for Heroes.

Deep in the building, in a massive area with two giant turbines that have obviously stood still for many years, a circle of seats is assembled.

A superhero is sitting on one of the seats, shuffling through notes and obviously in charge. She has long, flowing, very dark hair, and I'm most impressed to see she has what appear to be actual wings – like a bird's wings, but huge and dark brown. They flap slowly behind her, feathers bristling, as she reads. She takes out a pen and notes something in the margin of a page.

Four seats are vacant. The rest support nervous looking Heroes, wearing all sorts of colours and trying not to appear obvious as they check out one another's costumes. There is a girl who looks to be about eighteen years old, with three dots on her chest. Two middle-aged men are wearing matching black-and-white checked costumes. A guy who I'd guess is in his mid-twenties is wearing all purple. And I'm most astonished to see a kid about my age.

This kid is short and stocky and wearing a black bodysuit that looks to be baggy around the knees and shoulders, with a red circle with yellow flames on the front. He is also wearing red shorts, red boots with yellow trim that looks painted on, and he is sporting a big black crash helmet, like skateboarders might wear. A large bruise covers most of his cheek.

I take the seat next to him and sneak a sideways glance at his outfit. He's sneaking a glance at mine.

'Hi,' I say.

'Hi,' says the kid.

'Nasty bruise.'

'Pardon?'

'I said that bruise looks nasty. On your cheek. Are you OK?'

'Oh, yeah, I'm as happy as a bowl of water,' the kid says.

Eventually I have to ask, 'Is that happy?'

'Yeah, really happy,' he says, like I'm an idiot. Then reaches up to touch his face and winces in pain.

'Did you get the bruise fighting a super-villain?'

The kid shifts in his seat. 'Actually, I just got it. I smacked into the chimney arriving here.'

'Oh, that was you!' I extend a silver glove. 'I'm Ha – I mean, my name is Focus.'

The kid reluctantly shakes hands. 'Cannonball. Hi.'

We sit for a moment. I find myself wondering awkwardly what Heroes talk about.

Cannonball saves me by asking, 'So, you been a Hero for long?'

I think about lying but what would be the point? 'Actually, no. I only found out about a week ago. You?'

'Five weeks. Before that, I thought I was just a freak!'

'You did?' I can feel the relief flood through my body. 'I thought it was just me.'

Cannonball grins. 'I think everyone feels that way. That's why we're here, huh?'

And he's right. When the Bird opens the meeting, she explains that Heroes Anonymous is a non-judgemental forum for new Heroes: those who have just admitted they have powers or are having trouble admitting to being super people.

The two guys in black and white checks turn out to be the Crypto Twins – identical brothers where one has the power of only being able to talk in cryptic crossword puzzle clues, while his brother's power is that he's the only one who can understand him.

'Lo! The vulture lands messily, devouring a cross,' says one.

The Bird looks at his brother, an eyebrow raised.

'My brother says we are happy to discover we have powers but we're unsure how to use them,' he translates.

'It's a common issue for Heroes,' the Bird nods. 'It's one thing to discover you have powers; it is a whole different issue working out how, or even whether, to fight crime with those powers.'

'The church eats its mice,' announces the first Crypto Twin, nodding.

'Dot dot dot dash dash dash,' suddenly says the teenage girl with the dots on her chest. 'Dot dash dot. Dot dash dash dash dot dot.'

The Bird nods in encouragement and the girl, looking nervously at the other Heroes, finishes with, 'Dash dot dot dash dot dash dash dash dot dot dot dash.'

Me and Cannonball give each other looks. Cannonball shrugs.

'Miss Morse is right,' the Bird says. 'It can feel lonely being a Hero. What do you think, Berry Boy?'

The purple guy gulps. 'I've spent so long being considered a freak, I'm having trouble coming to terms with my power, which is that anything I cook ends up tasting like boysenberry.'

'Yet here we are, embracing our powers and our Hero selves,' says the Bird, spreading her wings for emphasis. 'Cannonball, that's a fine uniform you're wearing.'

Cannonball blushes. 'Thanks. I think it's even better than a crab. The lady at the superhero supply store made it for me. I chose the colour but she stitched it up.' He grabs a handful of material near his shoulder and shows how it bunches up in his hand. 'She made it with room for me to grow into, so it's a little loose.'

'That's fine,' says the Bird. 'You have years to become comfortable – with your costume and with who you are.'

Looking down at the clipboard where we had all written our names, she says, 'Focus, why are you here?'

I sit for a moment before I remember that she is talking to me. This dual-name thing is harder than you'd think, at least at first.

'Oh, um, sorry,' I say. 'Well, I'm only just getting started and I guess I wanted to be among some other Heroes and learn stuff.'

The Bird nods and gazes steadily at me, as I blur and unblur under her gaze. 'And have you tried any Heroic acts yet, Focus?'

'Not really. I went to the Car Crash thing in the car park but I was clueless. Unless HeroTV tells me, I don't know how to find criminals in action and, to be honest, I don't think I'd know what to do if I did.'

'Many Heroes team up when they're new to this life,' the Bird says. 'It can be a lot easier to work as a team, rather than go up against bad guys or attempt a rescue all by yourself. At least until you get your confidence.'

'How do you form a team?' Berry Boy asks.

The Bird shrugs. 'There's a classified section on herohints. com. You can advertise there. Or you can just network with Heroes you meet along the way. Speaking of which, let's break for coffee and then we'll do some training.'

'Beware the dog! It sings at Christmas!'

We all stare at the Crypto Twins.

'My brother says that's a great idea, he's thirsty,' explains the other Crypto.

'Boy, those two are going to confuse crooks into surrendering,' Cannonball whispers. 'They're as weird as a chimney.'

I'm pretty sure by now that Cannonball's power *isn't* making comparisons.

We all stand. The Crypto Brothers yabber at one another in their own language while Miss Morse heads straight for the coffee table. Berry Boy has beaten her there, already making himself a cup of tea, which he sips before saying to the Bird, 'Hmm, your tea tastes like boysenberry.'

Cannonball and I get biscuits and glasses of milk.

I say, 'Can I ask you something?'

'Sure.'

'What's your power?'

'My power?'

'Yeah, what do you do?'

Cannonball shrugs a bit too casually. 'Oh, you know, I can fly.'

I can't keep the admiration out of my voice. 'You can fly? That's awesome!'

'Yeah, well, you know, it's pretty cool.'

'I can't imagine anything better than flying.' My brain is ticking off all my favourite flying Heroes, scattered around my bedroom walls.

'It's not as great as you'd think,' Cannonball admits, touching the bruise on his cheek with a finger. 'And you, Focus? Is your power, you know . . .' He nods at the way I'm losing and gaining sharpness randomly.

'Yep, for what it's worth. So far, all I know is that if I get a fright I fall through walls.'

Cannonball laughs. 'Dude, at least you've got room for improvement.'

I find myself smiling. 'I sure have.'

Training turns out to be a whole new world of humiliation for me. The Bird takes us through some basic self-defence techniques and I realise I barely know how to throw a punch. I learn how to position my fist so it isn't sideways, which could lead to a broken wrist if I land a punch wrongly. I have no idea how to make a left jab roll into a right jab, and it turns out that you need to keep one foot behind you for balance, so that if somebody shoves you, you don't fall flat on your bum. I find this out the hard way with one decent shove from Berry Boy in a rare moment when I'm solid enough to shove. Everybody laughs.

'Don't worry,' the Bird says kindly, trying not to notice that my shaking hand passes straight through the hand she is offering to help me get back on my feet. 'It's your first day. It will become easier. Just don't go up against the bad guys yet. You need to train.'

CHAPTER 11
THE ALLEY OF DEATH

'm so depressed that I'm practically a cloud again. I fall easily through the solid wall onto the street and land on my hands and knees in the alley at the back of the power station.

'Well, what have we here? Where did you come from, little freak?'

I look up and I'm filled with panic. Stepping out from behind a collection of maybe a dozen big green wheely bins is a crazy-looking man, with a long, tangled beard and a nasty look in his eye. Dressed in a tattered coat and a beanie holding back his lank, grey hair, the guy has scars on both cheeks and a tattoo of a Frankenstein bolt on the side of his neck. He might be the most frightening person I have ever seen – including some of my school teachers.

I stand and try to look Heroic. In fact, I suspect I just

zap helplessly in and out of visibility. The man giggles – a manic, high-pitched giggle.

'Well, you don't seem to know whether you're here or not, little fella. The truth is, you'll wish you weren't, because I like the look of that silver cape thing you're wearing. I reckon that might make a good blanket. Hand it over, kid.'

I'm terrified. All my imagined first encounters with dangerous types had them cowering in the wake of my Heroic presence, not the other way around. But I'm also not happy about the idea of handing over my cape. That would be too humiliating.

I try to puff out my chest. I try to stop my focus wavering so wildly.

'Stay back and I won't hurt you,' I say, and wince at how high-pitched and squeaky my voice sounds.

The thug stares at me. And then throws his head back and laughs and laughs. I die a little inside.

'You won't hurt *me*?' he says, stepping towards me. '*You* won't hurt *me*! Well, that's good to know. Unfortunately, I can't make the same promise.'

He takes another ominous step forward and produces a steel bar from behind his back.

'In fact, I think there's a very good chance I will hurt you,' he says.

'I'm an Entry Level Hero, Grade Two,' I squeak miserably, taking a step backwards. 'You're not allowed to use weapons.'

The man giggles his high-pitched giggle again in the worst way. 'Yeah, that's what they say. But they're not here, are they?'

I gasp and take another step backwards, and that's what

saves me. My heel catches on something sharp, I stumble backwards and suddenly find myself on the other side of the wall, back inside the power station, a life-saving metre of brick between me and the crazy guy.

What really confuses me is the sound from the other side of the wall. It's like an urgent whistling with a kind of buzz behind it. It sounds far away but then very close, all in a rush. It finishes with a huge crash, the sound of rubbish bins bouncing in all directions, and then silence.

I sit there, frozen, panting with fear. I listen hard and finally I hear a voice on the other side of the wall say, 'Oops.'

I'm so shaken by the attack that falling back through the wall one more time is a no-brainer. With my shattered nerves, I wonder if I will ever be vaguely solid again.

A small figure in a baggy black bodysuit, red boots and a big black helmet is standing in the middle of the dark alley. Scattered bins are lying everywhere, and there, in the middle of them, the crazy guy is unconscious, the steel bar lying harmlessly beside his right hand.

'Cannonball! You saved me!'

'I did? I mean, yeah, I did!'

'How did you do that?'

Cannonball blinks at the still KO'ed man, and looks at me sideways. 'Um, well, . . . I saw you were in trouble and . . . Actually, I'm lying. I had no idea. The truth is, you know how I said I can fly? Well, it's true. I can. It's just that I have no control over it. I aim to fly somewhere but my body just takes off in any direction. I only fly a few metres off the ground and it usually ends when I crash into something. Crash hard. Like just now.'

'You weren't trying to fight this guy?'

Cannonball shuffles his feet. 'I was trying to fly home, which is that way.' He points off to the north. 'I had no idea you were even here. You're not exactly easy to see, no offence.'

We both stare at one another and then I feel a strange surge coming from my stomach. My entire body begins to shudder and I put my hands to my face. And then it erupts – a laugh. A wild, almost hysterical laugh of relief and disbelief. Cannonball's face splits into a giant smile and then he is laughing too. We laugh so hard I think I might die. My ribs are hurting from the laughter.

'You saved me and you didn't even mean to!'

'My first genuine superhero rescue! And it was completely accidental!'

'He had a steel bar. I thought I was dead!'

'I fly about as well as a tractor!'

We finally stop laughing, gasping for breath. Cannonball has the hiccoughs. The crazy guy moves his left foot slightly and murmurs.

'Quick,' I say. 'We have to get out of here before he wakes up. Fly while you can.'

'Actually, I think I've done enough flying for one night,' Cannonball admits. 'I'm going to get a taxi. I don't want to catch a tram dressed like this. Where do you live?'

'Northcote,' I say.

'Me too. Want a ride home?'

'I'd love one,' I say. 'I need to talk to you anyway.'

'You do?'

'Yeah, about joining my team.'

Cannonball stops and looks at me. 'You mean it?'

I had the idea as it came out of my mouth, but now I've said it, it feels right. 'You bet I do. I want you in the team. You in?'

I put out a silver-gloved hand, which is finally more or less physically there.

Cannonball takes it and shakes. 'You bet. I'd like that more than eating coal.'

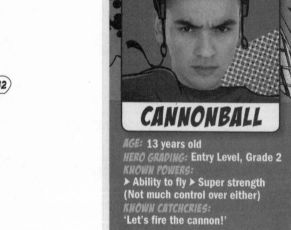

CANNONBALL

AGE: 13 years old
HERO GRADING: Entry Level, Grade 2
KNOWN POWERS:
▸ Ability to fly ▸ Super strength
(Not much control over either)
KNOWN CATCHCRIES:
'Let's fire the cannon!'

CHAPTER 12
WANTED: HEROES

Team members wanted.

Focus and Cannonball are looking for partners in crime-fighting.

Entry-level preferred. Girls as well as guys.

Nobody over 14 years old.

No vomiting powers, please.

(Must have own utility belt.)

'Look, we're sorry, but we don't think there's a place for you in the team.'

It isn't getting any easier, no matter how many times I break the news to wannabes who have replied to our advertisement on herohints.com, or heard about the auditions from a friend of a Hero friend, or maybe just wandered past the disused scout hall we're using. I don't want to sound superior, but there's no way half the kids we've seen have rated a visit from Leon or another Hero confirming they have powers, like I did.

This particular kid looks absolutely crushed.

'Oh,' he says.

'We think you're great, really great,' Cannonball says. 'It's just that we're not sure your powers adequately complement our own.'

'But fashion is everything in today's modern world.'

'Well yes, but we're not sure how it would apply to day-to-day crime-fighting. You'd fit into our team like a marble in a feather pillow.'

Bad Fashion Boy stands there, dressed only in his jocks, gumboots and rubber washing-up gloves, his eyes watering behind his snorkelling mask.

'So, anyway, sorry,' I say, opening the door.

'Well, good luck with the team,' Bad Fashion Boy mumbles. 'Let me know if you change your mind or need help with uniforms.'

'Oh, we will. Yes sir,' Cannonball lies.

I close the door and sigh. 'Jeez, this is horrible. He was even worse than Captain Snot.'

'And Unleaded Petrol Man.'

'We forgot to ask that guy how he actually discovered that his wee was unleaded petrol.'

'I hope nobody ever lights a match while he's going to the toilet.'

There is a sharp rapping on the door. I open it and there

stands a girl about two years younger than us, wearing a light blue skirt with several layers of light blue T-shirts. A light blue bandana ties back her hair.

'Hi,' I say. 'And you are . . .?'

'Yesterday,' says the girl dramatically. 'The Girl Who Can See Into the Past!'

'That's ridiculous,' I snort. 'You call yourself a Hero?'

'I knew you were going to say that,' she says, fingers to her temples and a mysterious look on her face.

'Actually,' Cannonball says apologetically, 'that's my little sister.'

To the girl, he says, 'Alexandra, I told you not to follow me here.'

'And I knew you were going to say that. By the way, don't use my alter ego name in front of strangers, *Nerdy*.'

'Cannonball,' he says through gritted teeth. 'The name is Cannonball.'

Yesterday and Cannonball are both standing, legs apart, hands on hips, glaring at one another. I can see the resemblance.

'So, um, Yesterday, why the blue costume?' I ask.

She shrugs. 'I like blue. And I knew that was the colour I was going to wear, once I chose it, because of my power.'

Cannonball says, as though in pain, 'You do not have a power. Everybody in the world can see into the past.'

'And everybody in the world can jump sideways too, fly boy,' she says. She puts her fingers to her temple again. 'Even the loneliest donkey walks the same path as the horse.'

'What does that mean?' I ask.

She opens her eyes and smiles at us. 'Whatever you want it to mean.'

'She thinks if she mutters deep sayings like that it will add credibility and mystery to her power,' Cannonball says, rolling his eyes. 'She's about as powerful as a hair dryer.' By now, I figure it's better just not to speak.

'So,' she says brightly, 'Who else is in our team?'

'You are not in the team!'

'I am too. Mum said not to leave me out of your games, remember?'

'This is not a game. This is serious.'

'Sure it is. Have you guys come up with a secret handshake yet? Oh wait, hang on.' She puts her fingers to her temple again. 'My power tells me you haven't.'

I say, 'Cannonball, can I have a quiet word, just for a second?'

We go outside and close the door. Cannonball slumps under his skater helmet.

'I'm sorry, Focus. She follows me everywhere. My mum is a nurse and single parent. She has to work weird shifts so Alexandra and I end up having to hang out.'

'You shouldn't call her Alexandra, you know,' I say.

'What?'

'Whether she's your sister or not, she's here in a costume and she says she has a power. We should respect her right to call herself Yesterday, just as we expect people to respect our Hero names.'

'She's about as much a Hero as an old carpet! She's just my idiot little sister.'

'So, we tell her to go home?'

Cannonball shifts his feet. 'Well, the thing is . . .'

I stare.

'We'll have to put in a lot of hours on this thing. And Mum will be furious if Al – I mean Yesterday – is left by herself for all that time.'

I can't believe this. 'So the third member of our team is only there because you have to babysit.'

'She might be useful. She could clean up our headquarters, get us drinks and stuff like that.'

'Oh, yeah, right. Are you going to tell her that, or will I?'

Cannonball puts his hand on the doorknob and looks back at me with a wicked grin. 'Hey, if her power's real, she'll already know and we won't have to tell her.'

Yesterday has a finger to both temples as we walk back in. 'Never sleep with a fish unless you've checked the water is clean.'

'I'll remember that,' I say.

The rest of the morning is no better.

Without fail, Yesterday says she knows each Hero isn't going to be accepted, the moment they leave the room.

One kid turns up and says his name is Freeze Frame.

'Uh huh?' says Cannonball. 'And what do you do?'

'This!' says the kid. He strikes a pose and freezes.

After about two minutes, nothing has happened. It doesn't even look as though he's breathing. We walk up to him and wonder what to do. Yesterday gently pokes his stomach.

'It's like he's a statue,' she says.

'There's nobody home,' adds Cannonball, peering into the frozen kid's eyes. 'He's as lifelike as calamari.'

We give it another five minutes. He doesn't move a millimetre.

'This is weird,' I say. 'What do we do with him?'

'Not to move can be very moving,' says Yesterday mysteriously.

Cannonball goes over and puts his stocky arms around the kid, then drags him into the far corner.

We leave him there, facing the wall.

A minute or so later, there is a soft, nervous knock and when we open the door, a kid is standing there, a little hunched, peering at us shyly from under a mass of long hair. He's about our age and his costume is a good one. Yellow and orange, with red flame-like shapes in the design, although it looks a little faded and frayed around the edges.

'Wow, nice threads!' says Cannonball.

'Thanks,' mumbles the kid. 'I, umm, inherited them.'

'What's your name, mate?' I ask.

'The Torch.'

'I knew that,' whispers Yesterday.

'Of course you did,' I say. 'So Torch, do you mean like THE Torch? The Flaming Torch? Is that what you do?'

'Sort of.' The kid looks at the ground and shuffles his feet, his face going red with embarrassment. 'Look, it's nothing much. I probably shouldn't have come. Sorry to waste your time.'

Cannonball raises his eyebrows at me. I shrug.

'You're here now,' I say, as the Torch turns towards the

door. 'You might as well show us what you can do. It's OK. We're all new to this.'

The Torch manages to raise his eyes to look at us for a moment and then mumbles, 'Well, OK, but like I said, it's not much. All I have to show you is this . . .'

And he clicks his fingers – in the process creating a spark of fire that glows off the bare skin on the index finger of his right hand with a steady glowing flame.

'Whoa!' says Cannonball, impressed.

'You ARE the Torch,' I gasp. 'Awesome! I've always loved Heroes who can burst into flame. You are SO in the team! Congratulations!'

The Torch blinks and blows out the flame so he can shake my silver glove. I can feel the heat from his finger.

'Wow! Really? I'm in? Are you sure?'

'Definitely.'

'You bet,' agrees Cannonball.

'I just knew you were going to be in the team,' says Yesterday.

'You know, the Flaming Torch has always been one of my favourite heroes,' I grin.

'He's my grandfather, but that's kind of a secret,' says the kid. 'He gave me the costume. My dad wore it for a while too.'

I'm peering at where the flame had been on the Torch's finger.

'Hey Torch, can I ask you one thing? I've always wondered – what happens to your clothes when you complete flame up your body?'

'Huh?' says the Torch.

'Come on, don't be shy! You know, when you yell "Flame on!" or "Fire!" or whatever you yell and your entire body bursts into flames. What happens to your clothes? Is your costume made of some special material?'

The Torch stares at me, gulps and then clicks his fingers again, so the tip of his index finger burns with its steady flame.

'Um, this is all I can do. I didn't say I got all of Grandad's powers. This is all that's left.'

We stare at his finger.

'You mean, the rest of your body doesn't catch fire?'

'Not even my other fingers. Just the index fingers on both hands.'

Cannonball snorts. 'Fantastic. We just let a human cigarette lighter join the team! Great work, Focus.'

The Torch looks crushed. 'I told you I was crap. Look, it's OK. I'll go. You don't want me in the team.'

I step between him and the door. 'Yes, we do,' I say, even though my visibility is fluctuating wildly as Cannonball gapes at me. 'All of us are starting out. None of us has the right to tell you that lighting flames, even if only off your fingers, isn't cool. I say you're still in.'

The Torch looks grateful. 'I can help in other ways. I know a lot about Heroes.'

'I'll bet you do. Cannonball?'

Cannonball sighs from under his big black helmet and says, 'I suppose he has got a good costume. What do you think, Yesterday? Am I going to want him in the team or not?'

Yesterday puts both fingers to her temples and scrunches up her eyes. 'You want him out!'

'Wrong again,' Cannonball says. 'Congratulations, candle boy. You're in.'

I never find out whether Cannonball only agreed to the Torch to spite his little sister.

'Time to knock off for lunch,' I say.

'Rest is useful only if you're tired, a wise man once said.' Yesterday is doing her temple thing.

'Yeah, whatever,' her brother says. 'Hey, what are we going to do with Freeze Frame?'

'Carry him outside and leave him?' I suggest.

So we do, dumping the statue kid frozen behind a poplar tree.

Feather Duster
REJECTED!

OK Team notes: Having a mop on her butt was briefly interesting, but is cleanliness crucial in a fight with villains? No.

The Grinner
REJECTED!

OK Team notes: Freaked us out after four hours of staring at us, never once dropping his grin. (Future politician?)

The Shredder
REJECTED!

OK Team notes: Eats bits of old paper. Limited use, and hate to think about when he goes to the toilet.

Super Backstroker
REJECTED!

OK Team notes: Great that he never hits his head on the end of the swimming pool when backstroking. Usefulness against arch villain? Zero.

Frisbee Boy

REJECTED!

OK Team notes: Had a fun hour playing Frisbee down the park, but not sure being able to throw a Frisbee is even a superpower.

Human Sewer

REJECTED!

OK Team notes: Ewwwwwwwww!

Glowstick

REJECTED!

OK Team notes: Looked impressive right up until the fourth minute when the batteries in his 'unearthly self-powered alien glowstick' ran out.

Flatulanto

REJECTED!

OK Team notes: Clear the room!!!!!

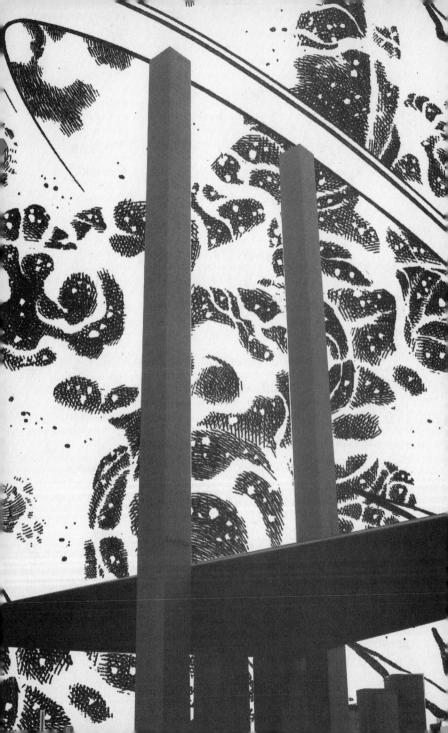

CHAPTER 13

THE GHOST &
THE LIAR

When we get back from lunch, Freeze Frame has gone. We have no idea where. He might have recovered and gone home. He might have been picked up by the garbage truck. We hope it's the former.

For almost the entire afternoon, the team membership stays at four. Sky Duck has a good costume (great feathers!) and strikes a dramatic pose.

'I am Sky Duck!' she squeals.

'And what exactly do you do?' Cannonball asks.

'When I look at the sky, I quack! Watch!'

She flaps her fake wings and looks steadily at us, her eyes wide and excited. The suspense builds. She flaps a little more quickly, then suddenly jerks her head to look straight at the roof.

'QUACK!' she yells.

'Next!' says Yesterday.

I'm pretty much ready to pack up when I see Cannonball look towards the door, and watch my friend's mouth fall open as though he's seen a ghost.

I turn around. Standing at the door is a small, pale kid with ghostly grey hair and red-rimmed eyes. He is wearing tattered, filthy-looking black pants and a dirty black shirt, with a black coat curled around him.

'Can I help you?' I ask uncertainly.

'Probably not,' says the kid. 'I am dead, after all.'

It takes me several moments to vaguely pull my own visibility back together, after the shock of seeing my very first ghost.

'That's not good,' I finally manage. 'I'm sorry to hear that.'

'I knew you were dead,' says Yesterday, fingers to temples.

'Well, I assume I'm dead. I haven't felt any need to breathe or to eat for more than sixty-three years.'

'Gee,' says Cannonball, in a voice that suggests even he thinks it's an inadequate response.

The dead kid shrugs. 'I'm kind of used to it by now.'

'Um, could you give us a moment please?' I edge away from the dead kid and march to the back of the hall, gesturing to the rest of the team to follow. Finally we are all in a huddle, even if I accidentally pass my arm through Yesterday's head as I struggle to recover my nerve.

As always, Cannonball gets straight to it. 'No way,' he declares. 'We are not having a dead kid in the group. That is weirder than an ice-creamery in a volcano.'

'It might just be me, but he's freaking me out and he hasn't even done anything,' Torch agrees, glancing over his shoulder to where the ghost remains in the doorway, staring intently at us.

'I sense you're against letting him join,' Yesterday says wisely.

'Is being dead even rated as a superpower?' I wonder.

'Well, I might be wrong but I believe there's Hellhound,' says the Torch. 'But nobody likes him.'

'I don't care if being dead is a power or not. I'm joining your group.' The dead kid is somehow right there, in the huddle with us.

Yesterday screams, then says, 'I knew you were going to do that.'

'I'm really sorry but we don't think there's a place for you in the team,' I say.

'I've been wandering aimlessly for sixty-three years. I'm bored. I want in.'

'What's your name anyway?'

'I dunno. I can't remember. I've been dead so long and nobody has called me by a name in all that time. I guess I'm just a dead kid.'

'That's the worst superhero name I've ever heard,' I say.

'Yeah, you need a better name,' nods Yesterday.

'Freak?' suggests Cannonball.

I feel myself blur in anger. 'We never, ever call anybody a freak, Cannonball. Got that? It's rule number one.'

'Who died and made you king? . . . Oh, sorry, dead kid.'

'What about Ghostly?' says Torch.

'Or Ghastly?'

'Ghost Boy?' says Yesterday.

'Ghoul Boy!'

'I've got it,' I say. 'Undead Fred.'

'But I am dead,' says the kid.

'Well fine. You can be Super Dead Kid.'

Cannonball has his arms folded. 'We seem to be missing the point here. Super Dead Kid, whatever you want to call him, is not in the team, unless he can prove he has an actual useful power, beyond the simple fact that he is dead. Sorry as we all are about that.'

There is a horrible silence.

'I can make blood come out of my eyes,' says Super Dead Kid, and does.

'Oh, that is so gross!' shrieks Yesterday. 'As a wise man once said, noble is the ghost who doesn't do disgusting things like that!'

'And I can pull my bones out of my chest,' says Super Dead Kid, and does.

'I'm going to be sick,' says Torch, lurching out the back door.

'They're not powers,' says Cannonball, unmoved. 'They're just wrong.'

'I'm sorry, mate, but Cannonball is right,' I say, wavering in visibility as I speak. 'If you don't have powers, you can't be in the gang.'

Super Dead Kid hangs his head. 'Oh well, I'll just wander the Earth for another sixty years then, or maybe 600,' he says as he turns and slowly walks out the door.

'Boy, now I feel horrible,' says Yesterday, 'even though, of course, I knew that was all about to happen.'

'Maybe his superpower is making people feel guilty?' Torch adds, still looking green.

SUPER DEAD KID

AGE: Uncertain
HERO GRADING: Not graded
KNOWN POWERS: ➤ No known powers beyond being the Living Dead
KNOWN CATCHCRIES:
'And you think your life sucks'

I'm just thinking that a whole day has gone by and the closest we've come to a fifth team member is an un-super dead kid, when the door to the hall swings open again.

Standing there, framed perfectly by the late afternoon light, is possibly the most beautiful girl I've ever seen. She's maybe fourteen years old, tall, and is wearing a purple velvet skin-tight costume and miniskirt, with a small cape drifting like a cloud off her shoulders. She has dark, long hair and grey eyes behind a small purple mask. I waver helplessly in and out of visibility.

Cannonball and Torch stand beside me, grinning stupidly. Yesterday strikes a pose, crosses her arms and scowls.

'Hi,' I say. 'Are you here to try out for our team?'

'No,' the girl says. Her voice is like pure honey.

'You're not? Oh, that's a shame . . . Given your costume I thought you might be a Hero.'

'No, I'm not,' she says.

Cannonball scowls. 'You have no powers?'

'Actually, I can fly,' she says.

'You can?' Torch gasps.

'Sure, and I'm bullet proof, have super strength, can outfly an Exocet missile, have X-ray vision, heat vision, can see into the future and shoot deadly lasers out of both hands.'

'Of course you do,' sniffs Yesterday, who can't help but look impressed.

We're all staring at the girl. 'Are you for real?'

'Absolutely.' She digs around in a purple bag that I hadn't even noticed she was carrying. 'Oh, and you're not supposed to read this.'

She hands me a piece of paper.

'To whom it might concern,
This letter is to confirm that the holder, Alison
Nomdeplume, has an unfortunate condition.

   The condition is such that she is unable to ever
tell the truth, in any circumstance. Absolutely any
statement she makes is a falsehood and should be
treated as such. Alison denies that the condition is a
medical one, which probably means it is, and she does
not believe that it could potentially be a superpower,
although we're not sure whether she is lying at this
point, despite the last sentence.

   Please regard Alison kindly as she has no control
over her complete inability to tell the truth.
Yours,
Dr Marvin Haywire
&
Ms Gwendoline Nomdeplume.'

We all read the letter four times.

   'Lying as a superpower . . .,' Cannonball says, removing
his helmet so he can better scratch his head.

   Alison adjusts a sleeve of her purple costume and then
produces a nailfile and starts rubbing a fingernail.

   'So, you can't tell the truth?' Yesterday begins.

   'That's wrong,' she says.

   'You have to lie, no matter what,' Torch adds. 'You can't
help it.'

   'Wrong again,' she nods.

'And your name is Alison Nomdeplume.'

'Yes.'

'Aha!' says Cannonball, looking pleased with himself. 'You just told the truth, after all.'

She gives him a dismissive gaze. 'Actually, I don't call myself Liarbird when I'm not being a Hero. And Alison Nomdeplume is certainly not a false name anyway.'

We all digest this.

'Also, did you know that if the world spun the other way, women would have beards?'

We're still staring.

'Look, I don't want to be in your gang so please don't tell me whether I'm in or not.'

'Give us one moment,' I say, pulling Cannonball by the shoulder to the other side of the room.

We go into yet another huddle.

'It's ridiculous,' I say.

'She looks familiar somehow,' says the Torch.

'All good hero teams have a babe!' grins Cannonball.

'Oh, please!' says Yesterday, rolling her eyes. 'How could she possibly be helpful? Excuse me if I've got this wrong, dear brother, but weren't you the one who argued against Super Dead Kid only five minutes ago, because he was useless?'

'That was completely different,' says Cannonball, looking shifty.

'How?'

'Well, she's alive and she doesn't freak us out, for starters.'

'She still can't actually help us,' says Torch, 'not that my opinion means anything.'

103

'She can handle public relations and media.'

I laugh. 'That's brilliant. But really, she shouldn't be part of the team.'

Cannonball looks crushed.

'I'm sorry,' I say to Liarbird. 'We're not sure your powers could be of any use to us.'

Just saying it almost kills me.

'I've got lots of money,' she says. 'I can pay for a decent headquarters, and a car for the team to get around in.'

'None of us have our licence. We're too young,' says Torch.

'I'll hire a driver, and buy in fast food when we need to work through meals.'

'That would be good,' I say.

'You know what else?' Liarbird continues. 'I'm close personal friends with lots of Triple A Heroes so I can get us all sorts of advice and introductions.'

'That's good enough for me,' I say.

'Yep,' says Torch.

'You bet,' says Cannonball.

Still fuzzy, I shake her purple glove. 'Congratulations, Liarbird, you're in.'

'Oh no,' she says, smiling.

'You do realise that everything she just said, about money and contacts and free food, were lies, don't you?' Yesterday scowls.

'Yeah. Whatever,' her brother says. Torch just grins like an idiot.

Yesterday shakes her head sadly. 'You guys are truly pathetic.'

CHAPTER 14
THE OK TEAM

Down a back street of Northcote we walk, side by side, united as a team, the sun glinting off our magnificent costumes. The yellow and red flames of Torch, then velvet, slinky, purple Liarbird, my silver and the light blue of Yesterday. Black helmeted Cannonball is stalking along on the outside.

I can't help but smile happily. I have no idea if we are any good but at least I have a team.

'Did you know that in Vietnam, they have dogs with eight legs that can chase nine balls at once? They keep them in igloos made of mud.'

'Fascinating, Liarbird. I'm sure they do,' says Yesterday. We've all come to know that Liarbird's habit of telling interesting facts allows her power to shine.

'And the Great Wall of China was built in three hours!'

'Interesting,' Yesterday sniffs. 'Now, back to the matter at hand. What about the Fantastic Five?'

'It's kind of almost taken,' I say.

'The Brilliant Five?'

'We don't know if we're any good yet, Cannonball.'

'So your idea is that we should call ourselves the Untested Handful, is it?'

'No, but I don't want to oversell ourselves. If we call ourselves the Amazingly Super Duper Incredibly Great Team, and then we don't win, we'll look like idiots.'

'I'm with Focus,' says Torch quietly. He rarely offers an opinion, too insecure to voice his thoughts. 'I think we should just hope that I'm OK and you're OK when it matters.'

'Have you read that book?' I ask him.

'Huh?'

'*I'm OK – You're OK.*'

'No,' says Torch, looking mystified. 'Sorry, boss. Should I?'

'Hey, who says he's the boss?' Cannonball wants to know.

'The Hopefully Not Too Bad Team?' says Yesterday. 'I sense that will be great.'

'Oh yeah, wonderful,' says Liarbird.

'I agree, Liarbird,' I say, edging closer to her. 'It's no good.'

We all stop. Unconsciously, we gather into a loose circle.

'What do we, in our heart of hearts, want to be?' Cannonball asks. It's a good question.

'We don't want to suck,' says Torch finally.

'Yeah, but we can hardly call ourselves that. The

"We Hope We Don't Suck Team".'

'We want to do OK,' I say.

We look at one another.

'The OK Team,' says Yesterday.

'I don't agree,' shrugs Liarbird.

'Not that my opinion matters but I like it too,' says Torch. 'Nicely understated.'

'I sense we might have our name,' Yesterday says, fingers to temples, eyes shut.

Cannonball is staring at us, disbelief all over his face. 'People! You've got to be joking! The OK Team? Just OK? We're superheroes. Some of us have capes! We have powers – well, not Yesterday, but you know –'

'Hey!' says Yesterday.

'If we aim low, we'll end low. What about the Cannonball Squad? Aiming for the sky.' Cannonball strikes a pose, and yells, 'Let's fire the cannon!' and then launches himself dramatically into the air. He slams into a wooden fence about twenty metres away, helmet dislodged.

'Oww.'

I turn back to the team. 'Let's be fair about this. We'll put it to a vote. Who votes for calling ourselves the Cannonball Squad?'

Cannonball staggers to his feet and raises an arm. The only other arm in the air is Liarbird's.

'I'll take that as a vote for no, Liarbird,' I say. It takes some work but I'm slowly getting the hang of catering for her 'power'.

'In Venezuela, when they hold an election, only the squirrrels get to vote,' she says.

Yesterday glances at her brother, her arm half in the air and then drops it back to her side.

'My own sister won't vote for my choice!' Cannonball says in disgust.

'I knew you'd be mad,' she says.

I ignore them. 'So, who votes for the OK Team?'

Yesterday, Torch and I raise our arms, even if my vote is almost void because I momentarily blur out of sight. Liarbird crosses her arms, which I count as a positive vote. 'Sorry Cannonball, but the vote stands.' I take a step towards my little black-suited friend. 'Come on, mate, at least we've got a team, hey?'

Cannonball sighs and shrugs. 'Oh well, I'm OK with that. The team name is about as important as a tail on a dog.'

'Is that important?' whispers Torch. 'I think it is, but maybe it's not? Has anybody got a dog? With a tail?'

Cannonball says, 'You know, I'll probably get too good for you losers anyway, and then it would be embarrassing if the team was named in my honour.'

'Yeah, lucky really that we went for the OK Team, now you think about it,' I say politely.

Newly named, the OK Team walks the streets for the first time. After a couple of kilometres, we haven't stumbled across the remotest sign of any crimes.

'Hey candle boy, I have a question.'

'I don't know much, Cannonball. I probably won't know the answer,' Torch replies.

'How do Heroes find bad guys mid-crime?'

'Oh, well, I have some idea about that, although I might

be wrong. Apparently, once you're a Triple A Hero you have some kind of super-pager, but the rest of us just have to cruise, keeping our eyes open.'

'Are you serious? Man, this could take weeks.'

Yesterday stops to check a blister on her heel from all the walking. 'And Torch, if Heroes are top secret and everyday people aren't allowed to know they exist, how come we can wander the streets in full view of everybody?'

Torch blushes, peeping out from under his hair. 'Well, again, I could be wrong and you're not going to like it if I'm right . . .'

'Just answer the question, he of the wondrous finger. Sheesh.'

'Well,' says Torch. 'Apparently, at this stage, Gotham can deny all knowledge of us. Until the OK Team starts recording some results, we're just a bunch of kids in Halloween costumes. If a member of the public claimed we were superheroes, they'd be laughed out of town.'

'Well, that doesn't suck,' says Liarbird. 'It reminds me of Spain, where at Halloween, children wearing superhero costumes are strung up by their thumbs between flagpoles and have bananas thrown at them.'

We roll our eyes at another 'Liarbird Fact', but agree that it is depressing. We trudge away from the main street and towards the school.

And that's when we hear the glass break.

CHAPTER 15

MEET THE BAD GUYS

'Holy tinkle!' says Cannonball. 'Did you hear that?'

I'm staring at him. 'Holy Tinkle?'

'I was just trying to set the mood.'

'I might be wrong but I think it came from the school,' says the Torch.

'It's probably nothing,' Liarbird says, peering through the fence.

'OK,' I say. 'This is what we've been waiting for, team. Let's get over that fence.'

We climb awkwardly, scrambling up the wire diamonds to scale the two-metre-high fence. I'm halfway up when it occurs to me exactly what I'm doing – climbing a fence to physically challenge my first genuine bad guys. I can't see Golden Boy turning up to a broken window at a school. This one's up to us. At which point, my body dissolves with fear and nerves and I fall clean through the fence.

Cannonball tries to fly over, but has barely finished shouting, 'Let's fire the cannon!' when he smacks nastily into a brick wall on the other side of the road. He staggers back and, after two more tries and collisions, grudgingly climbs the fence.

Another crash comes from the far side of the school. Whoever is doing the damage is still there. We look at one another with wide eyes behind our various masks.

'Is everybody ready?' I ask in a shaky voice. I'm still fluctuating wildly in my visibility.

Cannonball nods. Yesterday gulps. The Torch lights a finger.

Liarbird says, 'No.'

I put my silver glove out in front of me and hold it there.

'What are you doing?' Cannonball asks.

'We're a team. We need a pre-game catchcry. You ready? Repeat after me: I'm OK!'

They all look at me.

'Come on, put your gloves and hands on mine and say it when I say it, reply you're OK.'

Slowly hands and gloves pile on top of mine.

'I'm OK!' I say again.

'You're OK!' they all cry.

'Um, what I meant – oh, never mind. Now to finish, we all say, We're OK! Go!'

'WE'RE OK!', and we belt it out, loud.

'Cool,' I say. 'Let's get 'em.'

I've never been so scared in my life as when we come

around the corner of the shelter shed and find ourselves facing three teenagers at least three years older than us. Of course they're all built like footballers. Or professional wrestlers. Broad shoulders, muscled-up arms. My worst nightmare. One has long, heavy-metal unwashed hair. The other two heads are shaven. All have tattoos, and they don't look like the fake henna ones that some kids wear around to try and look tough.

One of the teenagers has a metal rubbish bin above his head, water sloshing out of it, about to hurl it through the science room window.

'Hey, stop that!'

I'm as surprised as everybody else to hear my voice. My visibility flares, fuzzes, then fades, as the three thugs turn slowly to stare at a bunch of costumed kids.

'You're trespassing and causing damage. You're under arrest.'

Even I can hear the tremble in my voice but I have to keep on with it. I try not to notice the sneer starting to creep across the three faces looking me up and down and mostly straight through me.

'We are Entry Level, Grade Two Heroes. What is your status?'

'Our wha –?' says one of the teens.

'You're kidding, aren't you?' says another.

'Our status is that we're gonna kick your butts,' says the third.

'Torch,' I hiss. 'They don't know about the Hero and Villain rankings. What does that mean?'

'I'm not sure about this, you know, but I think we're

supposed to hope there's a registered law enforcement officer on hand to negotiate the weapons and rules before we fight,' says Torch, looking even more scared than I feel.

But then Cannonball is next to us. 'You guys have got it wrong,' he says, confidently. 'If they don't know the rules then there are no rules. We can hit them with everything we've got. Rules are about as useful as buckets at a picnic.'

He swaggers to the front of our group, adjusting his black helmet and hitching up his baggy Hero pants. I have to admit that I envy Cannonball's fearlessness.

'You ladies ready to have your heads rearranged?' he asks the teens. 'Of course, in your case it would be a vast improvement, Ugly.'

The teen he is looking at processes this for a few moments then starts to scowl. 'Hey!'

'Yep, a brain like lightning,' Cannonball laughs. 'You want speed, I'll give you speed! LET'S FIRE THE CANNON!'

And with that, Cannonball strikes a pose, clenches his fists and launches himself to fly straight at the three surprised teen hooligans.

It takes a moment but finally I hear the bang behind us. Cannonball has landed hard, taking out a goalpost on the oval more than sixty metres away. 'Ouch,' he says, rubbing his ear.

One of the teens advances on what is left of the team. 'Well, that was entertaining, but I think it's time you bunch of freakoids got taught a lesson. This is a school, after all.' He walks up to the Torch. He's half a metre taller and twice as wide. Torch raises a trembling index finger and flicks it into flame.

'Thanks,' says the teen, producing a cigarette and lighting it. Then he flicks the cigarette at Yesterday, who squeals. The teen shoves Torch off to the side and swings a wild, roundhouse right-hand punch at me. Luckily I see it coming, completely dissolve in panic and barely feel the fist as it sails through the air where I should have been.

'I knew you were a bunch of thugs when we first saw you,' screeches Yesterday, glaring at the teen.

'Watch it, girlie.'

'Violence is the refuge of the coward,' she screeches.

'If I was you knuckle-draggers, I'd be looking forward to the full police SWAT team that is less than two minutes away.' It is Liarbird, arms folded, looking totally calm, defiant and, to my mind, absolutely gorgeous.

'Like, sure,' says the long-haired thug.

'You think we'd wander in here alone, you moron? You think a bunch of kids like us would be anything more than an advance party? We're the seekers and the heat is right behind us.'

'Gee, I can hear so many sirens,' says one of the teens.

'And I'm sure they'd send a SWAT team to deal with some broken windows.'

I find some clarity. 'We weren't looking for a bunch of young punks like you,' I say. 'Didn't you hear that the arch villain Monsterzoid was seen entering this school less than ten minutes ago?'

The boss thug snarls. 'Monsterzoid? Like the zit on your girlfriend's nose? That sort of Monsterzoid?'

Liarbird takes a step towards him. 'It's not a pimple on my nose, it's a mosquito bite. And we're talking about

Monsterzoid as in the alien life form that hides in rubbish bins and then shape-changes into liquid to drip onto his victim's heads and eat their brains from the inside.'

The thug with the steadily-dripping rubbish bin still poised over his head suddenly looks uncomfortable.

'And the same Monsterzoid,' Liarbird continues, taking another step forward, 'who continues through the victim's body until the water leaves via the usual channel, at a urinal, at which point Monsterzoid assumes human form, mid-wee.'

'Oh yuck,' says the boss thug, looking panicked.

'And the same Monsterzoid who is RIGHT BEHIND YOU!'

The three thugs gasp and spin, but of course there is nothing there.

'Nice try, hottie. But now you're really for it.' The lead thug advances on us.

Until a small pale shape appears right between them and us. Super Dead Kid pulls his own ghostly brain out of his skull, holds it up and says to the teens, 'Hi, I'm Monsterzoid. Who's got the tastiest brain?'

The three teens scream and run for it, disappearing towards the front of the school. At the same time, Liarbird grabs Yesterday and Torch by the arms and sprints off around the shelter shed. I scramble after them, wondering if Liarbird hadn't grabbed my arm because she might not be able to actually grab it, or because she cares about me the least? Mostly I wonder why I'm spending more time thinking about whether she likes me than the fact that I almost had my team pulverised by three teenage hoodlums.

Cannonball joins us as we reach the fence and we all go over or through it in record time, running fast from the school.

We are three blocks away before we slow down, wheezing and puffing.

'Well, that went about as well as I'd expected,' says Yesterday.

'I think we were brilliant,' Liarbird sighs.

A little ghost appears, standing next to the Torch who backs away slowly. 'You know what? You guys are so pathetic, I wouldn't want to join your team.'

'Wow, I love it when this little sweetheart turns up,' Liarbird says, recoiling.

'Oh, Liarbird, this is Super Dead Kid. He auditioned for the team before you,' I explain. 'Thanks for jumping in when you did, Super Dead Kid.'

'You're welcome. As a team, you do stink, though.'

'That's not constructive, all right?' I feel a need to defend the team. 'If you haven't got anything positive to say then don't say anything.'

Super Dead Kid thinks about that for a while and then shrugs. 'Fair enough. See you.' And he vanishes.

Torch looks uncomfortable. 'I don't want to cause trouble, but were we right not to let him join? He did better than any of us back there.'

Yesterday is scowling. 'But imagine hanging out with him every day. Yuck!'

'I agree, sis,' Cannonball says. 'He's too weird, even for us.'

'Put out your gloves,' I order, and they do, forming a stack of hands in the middle of our circle. 'Come on, I want us all to say our motto. That wasn't great, we've got room for improvement but, one way or another, we actually stopped some bad guys. We did have some success. There was some teamwork. Liarbird, you were great. We just need to train more.'

They all look unconvinced.

'I guess we did save the school, sort of,' the Torch says.

'I sense we will get better,' Yesterday adds.

Cannonball hangs his head. 'I sucked more than an icy pole. Big time.'

'It doesn't matter, mate. You had a crack,' I say gently. 'What do you say we have another audition? See if there are any useful heroes around to give us more firepower.'

'I don't know if anybody cares but I think that's a great idea,' Torch says. 'Strength in numbers.'

I gaze at my teammates, now at least meeting my eyes. 'Come on. Say the words.'

We all say together, 'I'm OK. You're OK . . . WE'RE OK!'

It is only later that it occurs to me that Liarbird, the girl whose power is an inability to ever tell the truth, has no problem saying the motto.

LIARBIRD

AGE: 14 years old (says she is 68)
HERO GRADING: Entry Level, Grade 2
KNOWN POWERS: ➤ Super-ability to NOT tell the truth (says her power is that she can eat planets)
KNOWN CATCHCRIES:
'That was a great idea'

CHAPTER 16
THE BIG SWITCH

That night, I place another advertisement on herohints. com for an audition to be held on the weekend. While I'm on the site, I notice a few less than complimentary descriptions of our recent 'battle'. The OK Team is obviously getting a reputation − a reputation for being the most pathetic outfit around.

The auditions are a disaster. The Human Sprinkler is the worst. He starts by drinking eight litres of water, which is *a lot*, then looks at photos of waterfalls and turns on a hose so it trickles next to him. Finally, he spins around in circles for more than five minutes until he is totally giddy. He has only just begun to drop his trousers when he is forcibly led from the building by Cannonball and the Torch.

Nobody else even turns up for a couple of hours until a lanky kid walks in the door.

'I am the Flying Saucer!' he declares. He is wearing a green bodysuit with an oversized Mexican bandit ammunition belt around his waist and another flung over his shoulder, and a sombrero on his head. The ammo belts are full of what appear to be plastic bottles with spouts.

'What's with the hat?' asks Cannonball.

'Hey, you wear a stupid helmet, I wear a sombrero,' says Flying Saucer.

'O-kay,' I say. 'You say you can fly, huh?'

'A-ha! Wrong again!' declares the teen. 'I only said I am the Flying Saucer!'

'I can't wait to have you in the team,' says Liarbird.

'Thanks, toots. I can't wait to get to know you either.' Flying Saucer gives her an exaggerated and very obvious wink.

'Ugh, that's not gross,' Liarbird gasps.

'Is there any chance you can show us what you can do, if anything?' I say, gritting my teeth.

'Sure, fuzzy,' says Flying Saucer and crouches. 'OK, say that big human-shaped pile of cardboard boxes is a bad guy, right?'

'Which would be why we made it human shaped and placed it in front of you . . .' says Yesterday.

'Yeah, whatever,' he says. 'Watch this.'

He flexes his fingers near his hips like a gunslinger, and then suddenly grabs two bottles off his belt and splurts green liquid from one and red liquid from the other onto the cardboard villain. 'Take that! And that!'

We all stare blankly, arms folded.

'He splurts sauce,' whispers the Torch.

'Flying Sauce!' says the kid. 'In this case, green tomato sauce and Mexican chilli sauce.'

I sneak a glance in Liarbird's direction. She starts to smile and I do too. Our eyes lock, enjoying the moment, but it's interrupted by Yesterday saying, 'Well, stringbean suit. If we're ever having a barbeque, you'll be the first one we call . . . after Soft Drink Dispenser Man.'

'Who?' says Flying Saucer.

'He was in earlier. Sorry, mate, you're not what we're after.'

'Fine, have it your way. I'll form my own stupid team!'

'You might want to look up the Ketchup Kid,' says the Torch quietly.

Flying Saucer doesn't hear him, stomping out.

'Torch!' Cannonball says. 'Was that a joke? Thrown in the actual direction of a stranger? You're getting brave!'

The Torch blushes. 'I'm not really big enough to say this, but go eat your cape, demolition ball.'

'Listen, you walking cigarette lighter . . .'

'And you losers wouldn't let me join your team,' says Super Dead Kid, suddenly appearing and shaking his pale head. 'Yet look at who you're prepared to audition.'

'Yikes! I hate it when you just apparate in the middle of us,' yelps Yesterday.

'Shouldn't you know I'm about to arrive?' says the ghost, leering at her.

'That's not the point, Super Dead Kid,' Yesterday fumes. 'Knock at the door if you want to come in.'

'What's the fun of being the walking dead if I have to knock on doors?'

'All the other ghosts do,' says Liarbird. 'We had three here yesterday and they all knocked.'

'Oh, please!' says Super Dead Kid, but he disappears.

There is a knock on the scout hall door.

'Get lost, Super Dead Kid!' yells Cannonball.

There's another knock, a little louder.

'I said, go shove your stupid ghostly head!'

The third knock shakes the door.

Cannonball strides over and flings the door open. 'For the last time, you annoying little phantom – oops.'

It's not Super Dead Kid standing at the door. It is a Hero – a real Hero.

More than two metres tall, the man is a rippling ball of muscle, wearing a brilliant black and white uniform, with a truly heroic, fashionably-shaped cape blowing behind him as though he has his own wind machine. He's wearing a striped mask with thin bands of green, yellow, blue, red, purple and orange and black.

'Wow!' Yesterday exclaims. 'I mean, I knew he was about to arrive.'

'Who are you?' I ask as he steps into the scout hall, Heroically filling the space.

In a voice like distant thunder, like powerful waves crashing on rocks, the Hero says, 'I am Switchy.'

We all stare until Cannonball snorts. 'Switchy?'

'That's 300 per cent right,' the Hero says, turning to tower majestically over Cannonball. 'Switchy. You got a problem with that?'

'Um, no . . . sir.'

The Torch shuffles forward with an appraising eye,

moving close to the Hero, almost sniffing at him, like a dog. 'I might be wrong, because what do I know? But I think you're a changeling,' he says.

'That's 220 per cent right,' says the towering Hero. 'I switch.'

'Torch?'

The Torch turns to face me, smiling from under his hair. 'He can be anything! His power is that he can change how he looks, who he is. Very cool! There are different names for people like him . . . You might have heard of shape-shifters.'

'Wow,' says Yesterday. 'I always thought they were just mythical.'

Liarbird grins. 'I'm not impressed. Let's throw him out now.'

'Huh?' says Switchy, looking hurt.

'Don't worry, you'll get to know her,' I say. I turn to the others, eyes shining. 'I say he's in, gang. What do you think?'

Everyone agrees, nodding furiously, except for Liarbird's shake of the head.

'Congratulations, Switchy, you're just what we need,' I say. 'Welcome to the OK Team.'

'Awesome. That is 400 per cent for sure the best news I have ever heard in my entire life. Thanks a lot,' says Switchy.

'Feel free to ignore me if this is too much trouble, but could you please show us a change?' the Torch asks.

'Um, OK,' says Switchy. He frowns mightily and holds his breath until his handsome face turns red.

'Is he doing a poo?' asks Yesterday quietly.

'Shhh,' says her brother, shoving her.

Switchy's face turns red and his massive body trembles, but then there is a pop and standing in front of us is a tall, very skinny kid about fourteen years old. He has bright red hair, freckles and is still wearing the striped mask over his eyes.

'What's this shape supposed to be?' says Cannonball.

'Um, I think it's me,' admits Switchy, no longer with the deep, impressive voice.

I blink. 'This is you? Then what was before?'

'A shape.'

'Go back to that shape.'

'I'll try.' Switchy holds his breath again, goes through the whole painful build-up, and there is another pop.

In front of us is a washing machine with a striped mask around its control buttons.

'Did you mean to do that?' asks the Torch.

'Don't change back,' Liarbird says.

The washing machine appears to tremble and changes from white to a slight shade of pink, then there is a pop and a stripey-masked cow stands in front of us.

'Switchy?'

'Moooooooo.'

It holds its breath, shakes and pops back into the gangly kid version of Switchy, looking a little embarrassed.

There is a silence.

'So, you have no control over what you change into,' I finally suggest.

Switchy looks at the floor and self-consciously scratches

his right arm with his left hand. 'Sometimes I get it right.'

'How often is "sometimes"?' Cannonball wants to know.

'Once in a while. Maybe every tenth time. Or twentieth.'

'And you only *think* this particular shape is actually you?'

'It's sort of complicated,' he says.

'Oh, great,' Liarbird groans.

'I told you he'd be crap,' Yesterday says.

The Torch whispers to me and I nod. 'You're right, Torch, he's no worse than the rest of us and he *might* turn into something handy when we need it. You still want in, Switchy?'

Switchy's face shines under his multi-coloured mask. 'That is 1423 per cent correct! I definitely, absolutely and completely want in!'

From the *Hero Times*:

ROOKIE HERO TEAM NOT OKAY

Melbourne, yesterday (AHP*):
Australia's newest Hero outfit, The OK Team, has had yet another blow - to the team-members' bodies as well as their self-esteem. The OK Team has now had its butt kicked five times, always by criminals and Villains so low on the rankings, if in fact they rate as actual Villains, that they are not recognised in any database of good or bad guys.

The latest incident involved a couple of pre-teen girls allegedly shoplifting at a convenience store. Cannonball managed to knock himself out with a full-blooded frontal assault that saw him demolish the brick wall of a church across the road. Switchy did his best by turning into a small dog, yapping around everybody's feet, but the under-age Villains disposed of the rest of the team with stolen water pistols.(*Associated Hero Press)

From the *Daily Cape*:

CYCLIST RIDES RINGS AROUND NEW TEAM

Melbourne, this morning (AHP): The OK Team failed again today, with an unsuccessful attempt to halt a lone bike thief at the local library. The thief disposed of the Torch by pushing him into Switchy, who had started proceedings by helpfully changing into a charity clothes bin. "I sensed that the Torch was destined for trouble," said Yesterday, the Girl Who Can See Into the Past, "but the rest of the team were too busy trying to help him squeeze back through Switchy's metal lid to listen."

Team leader, Focus, told the Daily Cape he was confident his team was close to success. "We're getting better at our moves. We remain committed and optimistic. A win is just around the corner," he said. At least, it was believed to be Focus. The speaker was practically invisible while facing sceptical reporters.

OK TEAM LEADER DEAD!

By Staff Reporters

Melbourne, today: Focus, the young leader of Melbourne's inept OK Team, is apparently dead. Punched in an altercation with a dog walker yesterday, the visibly challenged rookie Hero has unexpectedly died of his injuries.

Team member Liarbird told reporters that Focus had suffered terribly from wounds including gangrene in the left leg, nine broken or missing ribs, a dislodged head, and a large anvil embedded in his neck. AFHT executives were on their way to OK Team headquarters to assess the situation at the time of going to press.

ENOUGH IS ENOUGH, SAYS GOLDEN BOY

Australia, Tuesday: Australia's leading Triple A Hero, Golden Boy, has questioned the international rules for allowing active Hero participation. "I'm not against Heroes having a go. In fact, some of my best friends are wannabe-Heroes, but at some point we need to ask whether it is useful to have ill-equipped, under-powered try-hards on the street," he told a press conference.

"There are teams out there right now who will get badly hurt or hurt somebody else through their lack of experience, crime-fighting ability and intelligence. Some of these kids are only fourteen or fifteen years old. They have dubious powers at best, and no obvious leadership or strategy." It is believed Golden Boy was alluding to a recently debuted line-up, The OK Team, which has suffered nine straight losses against a variety of low-level opposition, including members of the public with no actual evil powers.

But fellow local Hero, the Ace, said he thought Golden Boy was dealing lesser Heroes a rough hand. "It's OK for an all-powerful Hero like Goldie, who has been dealt a royal flush when it comes to ability. But others don't have the same trumps. I think you can only play the cards you are dealt, and these kids are doing just that."

OK TEAM LEADER NOT DEAD

Melbourne, 18.30 hrs (IntHP): AFHT officials have confirmed rookie Hero, Focus, is only suffering a bruised cheek, and was not actually killed in the team's latest setback. The barely visible newcomer to Hero ranks managed to regain his physical shape just in time to cop a punch from a dog-walker who had omitted to clean up a dog poo in a Northcote park recently.

"It's good to see Liarbird's power coming along nicely, but reporters might like to remember her talent when asking her for quotes in future," said leading local Hero, Southern Cross.

CHAPTER 17
GAME OVER

e're sitting in the Vegie Bar, the only place I could be sure nobody would look twice at us. We've just been left humiliated by six ten year olds running rampant through the local streets on a sleep-over birthday party.

Any way we look at it, we are hopeless. Every night, on Channel 78737, I watch story after story from around the world of Triple A rated Heroes performing the most astonishing rescues, captures and Earth-saving feats. Occasionally a B or C rated Hero is applauded for punching above his or her weight. One night, a D rated newcomer saves a car from an oncoming train, through ingenuity and muscle.

I can't even make a guy pick up after his dog. The team's success rate stands at zero wins, fourteen losses. Lurch gives us a long, long look as he takes our order, then raises an eyebrow in my direction before walking silently away.

Cannonball is holding a wet hankerchief to the lump on the side of his head. The garage door he unintentionally slammed into is feeling worse.

'How can we be so crap?' he rants, following a familiar theme. 'We were worse than crap. We were mega-crap. We redefined crap. We're more crap than a pile of horse poo. We completely reinvented the word crap. If you built letters to describe us that were big enough to cross the Nullarbor desert, they would read "Crap".'

'Cannonball, give it a rest,' I say. 'You're not helping.'

'Crap! Ultra ultra ultra ultra crap.'

Yesterday is slumped at the table next to her brother. She spent the whole battle with the ten year olds yelling, 'Don't you dare hit my friends! Oh, I KNEW you were going to do that! I'm really mad now. I know you're about to try and hit me so I'm going to run. VIOLENCE DOESN'T SOLVE ANYTHING!'

The last bit was yelled over her shoulder as she bolted from the scene.

Liarbird, now putting a Bandaid on a scraped elbow, still with garbage in her hair from where the birthday girl tipped a rubbish bin over her, says, 'The good news is we're getting better. Did you know the only team to be better than us was the Bare-Bottom Four who waved their bums at bad guys for six months in Turkey, before being arrested for unseemly behaviour?'

I'm glad I can discount that as a 'Liarbird Fact', because it would be simply too depressing if it was true.

The Torch just sits, head down, in his own little world of pain. He'd frozen through the entire battle, apparently unable to garner the confidence to even attempt an attack after so many OK Team disasters.

Switchy is currently in the shape of an iPod, sitting quietly next to my elbow on the table.

'Crap,' says Cannonball again, just in case anybody missed it before.

I feel a surge of anger. Without thinking, I lash out and try to punch the wall, only to watch in frustrated amazement as my fist passes straight through the band posters plastered there. I'm so hopeless that I can't even manage a classic display of temper.

Lurch approaches with our drinks. He gives us another look.

'Team,' he says.

'You know we're a team?' I stand to be slightly closer to Lurch's face, way above. 'I knew it! I knew you were one of us.'

Lurch looks at me for a long time, then at the team members, one after the other.

His gaze fixes on Torch. 'Team,' he repeats. 'Family. Holds the key.'

He walks away, and I stare after him.

'Cannonball?' Liarbird says. Everybody looks up because it probably means she wants to talk to anybody other than Cannonball.

She is looking at me, but struggling to meet my gaze, which has never happened before.

'What is it, Liarbird?'

'I'm thinking that we should keep trying, because we're sure to improve.'

(133)

There is total silence.

'You want us to quit?'

'No,' she says quietly. 'I don't think we are wasting our time.'

I put both hands to my face, glad that they don't pass through my skin. I feel numb. It's over. Is it over? It might be over.

I finally look up and see the others gazing steadily at me, except for Cannonball who has the wet hanky across his face and isn't moving a muscle. The Torch looks like he is holding his breath.

'What do the rest of you think?' I ask, my voice unnaturally high.

'We are pretty crap. I always knew we would be,' says Yesterday.

'You want out?'

'I don't want out, but I think Liarbird might be right for a change. As a wise man once said, "Foolish is the man who walks uphill beside a chairlift".'

'Torch?'

This is the most intense moment we've shared. Torch shrugs miserably, unable to talk.

'Switchy?'

The iPod makes a faint sound. I pick up one of the ear plugs and can hear The Beatles' song, 'Ticket to ride'. I don't know whether that's a yes or a no.

'Cannonball?'

'I'm not quitting.'

I could kiss him.

'You're still in?'

'Of course I'm still in.' Cannonball finally moves the hanky and sits up straight. 'You all thought we'd just turn into IncredoMan overnight? Put on a mask and away we go? I'm in this for the long haul and I don't care how many garages I crash into.'

I feel a burst of pride, until Cannonball adds, 'What the rest of you losers do is up to you.'

'Well, I'm not quitting either,' I say. 'And you know what? I'm not quitting on the OK Team. I believe in us. I like hanging out with you guys,' (some more than others, I think to myself, working hard not to look at Liarbird), 'and I say we keep going. Before too long, we'll be giving a bunch of delinquents like we faced today a real kicking.'

'They were pretty tough, for under twelves,' Yesterday admits. 'I'll bet higher grade heroes than us would have had trouble with them.'

'Yeah, right,' snorts Liarbird, arms crossed and giving Yesterday her most withering glance.

Yesterday cocks her head to one side. 'What's with the look, fib-face? Even without my superpowers, you'd be *so* obvious.'

'And an excellent power you have too,' snaps the girl in purple.

'You two, please,' I say, and am surprised to find I'm hardly out of whack at all. 'Give us a couple more weeks. We're just missing one thing, and I think I know what it is. Torch, you still with us?'

'I guess,' he says, muttering from somewhere near his knees. 'Not that I'm worth anything. It doesn't matter if I tag along or not for all the good I do.'

'I disagree, Torch. Lurch said something about family holding the key, and I think he meant you. Tell me more about the Heroes in your family.'

The Torch shrugs. 'There's not much to tell. My great-grandfather and my grandfather could both flame up completely. My dad can only light up his left foot, which is such a useless ability he hasn't actually done it for years. My uncle occasionally finds his eyebrows smouldering, but that's about it.'

'Is your grandfather still alive?'

'Yeah, sure. He lives two suburbs away.'

'Can we go and visit him?'

'What, now?'

'Yeah, it's important. All of us. As a team. Liarbird? Yesterday?'

Liarbird shrugs and says, 'I've got better things to do, especially since my application to be an astronaut with NASA has been accepted. I leave on Tuesday.'

'I sense we're going to see Torch's grandpa,' Yesterday declares.

I turn to Cannonball. 'You in, mate?'

Cannonball sighs and shakes his head. 'You guys are luckier than a green pelican to have me on board. Just don't take it for granted is all I'm saying.'

'Was that you speaking, or Liarbird?' Yesterday asks, and has to duck as her brother takes a swing at her.

CHAPTER 18
THOSE WERE THE DAYS

'Of course, villains were real villains back then. You couldn't afford to be squeamish when you were facing down the Bloated Alien Rubbish-Monsters of Broome's outer suburbs. Nothing but you and some pure flames between them and Western Australia's top tourist destination. In fact, that reminds me of another story – the time I had a super team-up with Amazing Anzac to save a busload of tourists from a nasty flood in Queensland. He was a character, that Amazing Anzac. Old AA was the only Hero I ever knew who could keep his slouch hat on his head no matter how long he was dangled upside down and shaken by an oversized gorilla. He once said to me, "The young Heroes these days, Torchey . . . they just don't respect the history of the art." And he was right. I remember . . .'

I sip my cup of cold tea and try to look interested. Next to me, I can feel Yesterday fidgeting. Liarbird is simply staring at the Torch's grandfather, perched in his big chair, rug over his knees, occasional whiffs of smoke rising off his hands as he reminisces about the old days. He's been talking now, stopping only occasionally to breathe, for more than forty-five minutes.

But the most intense heat is coming from Cannonball's gaze, boring into me from the chair across the room. I'm very careful not to look in that direction.

'Um, excuse me, Grandpa Torch,' I finally manage.

'You can call me Papa Torch, young man. That's what they used to call me in 1944 when I was in Singapore. I remember one day, I think it was a Thursday, no, maybe it was Wednesday. It was steamy, I remember that, and –'

'Papa Torch,' I say. 'We have something to ask you. A favour . . .'

'Very steamy. You needed superhero deodorant during that campaign, I can tell you. Poor Jelly Girl was utterly –'

'Papa Torch,' I say, almost sharply.

'Eh? What?' the old man squints.

'We have something to ask you. A favour . . .'

'Me? A favour? What can an extinguished human campfire like me possibly do to help you young'uns?'

I take a deep breath and say it. 'We need you to coach us so we can become better.'

I can feel my teammates' eyes swing onto me as one. I might even hear a horrified gasp. I can imagine Liarbird's voice saying, 'That's an excellent idea.' But I'm hoping that if I make it sound like coaching a team, Papa Torch might forget that we're his grandson's random bunch of uselessly powered mates.

Papa Torch scratches his knee where it is slightly smouldering. 'Coach?'

'We don't know what we're doing. We're a bunch of kid Heroes who mean well but have no idea where to start or how to improve. We need someone who was once a Triple A Hero to teach us how to play in the big game.'

Papa Torch is shaking his head. 'No, no, no, young Locust.'

'Focus, Sir.'

'Eh?'

'Focus, Papa Torch. It's Focus.'

'I am focusing, young man, but I don't think I can help you. I only know about flames, about my own power. Young Torchy, my favourite grandson, I might be able to help. But you lot, with your –' he waves an old, saggy-skinned arm in the direction of Cannonball, then Switchy, who is currently a refrigerator '– with your powers of flying, and changing, and shooting goldfish out of your eyes, and being able to lie down with birds . . .'

We all stare at him.

'. . . well, I don't know much about any of that. You see, being a Human Torch is a very specific skill set. You have to learn how to flame on. You have to learn how to flame off . . . That's pretty much it, I think. Oh, hang on, no. There's clothes to think about. Temperature and outside weather conditions. Heavy rain etiquette. Marshmallow factory crimes need heat considerations. Um . . .'

'So you can't help us,' I say, sagging.

'Nope,' the old man says. 'Although . . . I could tell you some stories.'

'No, really, that's not necessary,' I say hastily. 'We'd better be going anyway.'

The team stand and say their half-hearted, uninterested goodbyes. Nobody will meet my eyes, which I don't take as a good sign. Even Cannonball has stopped trying to stare me out. I've rolled one last dice and it's come up with the wrong number.

Liarbird is the first to leave, followed by Cannonball. Yesterday and Switchy, now a clown, wave on the way out. Torch hangs by the door, as I thank the old man for his time.

'No problem, young fella. Always good to talk to up-and-coming Heroes. You'll be right. Great team you've got there.'

'I'm not sure I have got a team any more,' I say.

But the old man is squinting again, as though trying to see an important fact on the other side of the room. 'You know, I suppose I could call Fab.'

'Who?'

Torch is suddenly smiling. 'Grandad! Are you serious?'

'He's coaching now. That's all he does. He'd love to come to Australia, I'm sure. Has a lot of mates here.'

I'm still looking blank.

'You've got to work on your Hero history, son,' says Papa Torch, reaching for some extremely old comics in a bookshelf near his chair. 'Here. I want these back, but you read them before he arrives.'

I say, 'You mean, THE Mr Fabulous?'

Torch appears at my shoulder and says, 'Oh boy, this is going to be fun. Focus, we are SO back in the game.'

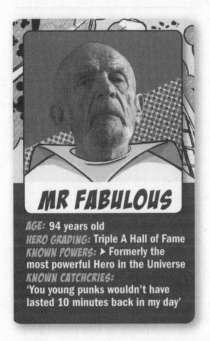

MR FABULOUS

AGE: 94 years old
HERO GRADING: Triple A Hall of Fame
KNOWN POWERS: ▶ Formerly the most powerful Hero in the Universe
KNOWN CATCHCRIES:
'You young punks wouldn't have lasted 10 minutes back in my day'

CHAPTER 19
MR FABULOUS

Cannonball's arms are folded across his chest.

'So if this guy is, like, one of the most legendary of all Heroes ever, how come he has to fly Qantas to Australia?'

I sigh. 'I've told you, Cannonball. He's incredibly old. He was a Hero back in the original Golden Age in the late 1930s and early 1940s, sixty or more years ago. His powers have faded over time. He could maybe manage to fly under his own power, if he could island hop across the Pacific, but he convinced Gotham to pay for a flight.'

'To help us? Gotham is paying for him to come and help a bunch of losers like us?'

I turn and grin at my friend. 'Believe it or not, popgun. Something called the Underachieving Trainee Hero Assistance Scheme.'

'The acronym for that is L.O.S.E.R.S.'

'No it isn't, Liarbird. Travelling around and helping teams like us is how Mr Fabulous earns his living these days.'

We all stand and watch as some tourists emerge from the arrivals gate, then a couple who are immediately caught up in shrieks and hugs from an excited wider family.

I frown. 'Do you know what he looks like, Torch? Will you recognise him?'

'I can only hope I don't make some horrible mistake, but I think I'll recognise him. Don't you worry,' Torch says. He's been more animated than I've ever seen him from the moment Mr Fabulous confirmed he was on his way.

'Some old mouldy piece of Hero history is going to be just what we need to sort out our absolute brilliance when facing bad guys.'

It is Liarbird again, and everybody has to digest and translate.

'Let's wait and see, Liarbird,' I say. 'This guy is an all-time Hero. An original Hall of Famer. What can we lose?'

I look at her, slightly pleading, and she looks right back at me, the beginning of a smile on her lips. Suddenly I'm having trouble remembering the Hall of Famer's name.

'Torch, I sense you're about to say, "There he is",' says Yesterday dramatically.

A huddled old man, more wrinkles than skin, has emerged from the gate. He is wearing a massive overcoat, with loose threads and patches, as well as a giant cowboy hat that can't quite hide the fact that the grizzled old face below the brim is wearing a faded blue mask. Beneath the coat can be seen blue boots, scuffed and of an uneven colour, and the end of a yellow cape dragging behind his feet. He is leaning hard on a stick and carrying one small suitcase.

'There he is!' says Torch.

Yesterday looks smug but Cannonball finds time to hiss to his sister, 'Oh please, he was already out the gate.'

'You are so unsupportive.'

We walk over and catch up to the old man beside a large rubbish bin.

'So, are you lot the young punks who can't cut it in the real world?' he says.

'Mr Fabulous?' I say in reply.

'Oh sure, shout it to the whole world, why don't you, sonny. Ever heard of discretion?'

'Umm, sorry.'

'It's okay.' He looks around, warily. 'I don't think anybody saw through my cunning disguise anyway. No autographs – that's rare. Maybe Australia is a good place for me to hang out. Get some peace from the usual crowds of fans.' He looks at us for the first time, appraising. 'So you're such a big fan of mine that you've taken to wearing my "F" on your chest, huh?'

'Actually . . .' I say, but the old man isn't expecting a reply. He's moved on.

'You look like a chip off the old Torch flint,' he's saying. 'Am I right?'

Torch sneaks a glance in each direction but nobody is watching, so he flicks a flame onto his right index finger.

'Hey, hey, hey. Look at that! How's your grandad, sonny?'

'He's great. He's looking forward to seeing you.'

'Let's go now. Drop these losers.'

'Um, but they're my teammates . . .'

Mr Fabulous squints at him.

'. . . that you're here to help,' Torch adds lamely.

'Oh yeah. Sorry, I forgot. So who are you punks again?'

I decide to step back in.

'I'm Focus, sir. My real name is —'

'Don't tell me your real name! For crying out loud, ever heard of a secret identity? For pete's sake!'

I decide to shut up for a while.

'Cannonball, sir.' Cannonball puffs out his chest and plants his hands on each hip. 'Let's fire the cannon!' he says.

'You've got to be kidding,' says the old man. 'That's your tag line? Boy, have we got some work to do. Who are you, darling?'

He's looking at Yesterday.

'I'm Yesterday, Mr Fabulous, the Girl Who Can See Into the Past. It's lovely to meet you.'

'The girl who can see into the past,' he says very deliberately.

'Weary is the head that puts suspicion ahead of belief. I'm also Cannonball's sister.'

Mr Fabulous nods wearily. 'OK, a brother-sister act. I can work with that, girlie. Gives me some bones to build on, plus Focus and Torchy. That's it, huh?'

'Um, you haven't met Switchy,' I say.

'Switchy? What the hell kind of superhero name is Switchy? What does he or she or it do?'

I can barely bring myself to say it. 'He's a shape-shifter. Switchy, you might want to change.'

The rubbish bin we are all standing next to suddenly begins to shake slightly and turns a strange pink colour before making a loud pop and turning into a Vespa scooter. Then pops again and becomes a giant squid, then pops a third time and becomes a large nose, filled with snot. Finally, it pops and turns into Switchy.

Mr Fabulous stares at him for the longest time before saying: 'Ohhhhhh, boy. Good morning, Switchy.'

'You can bet everything you own that I'm pleased to meet you, sir,' says Switchy.

The old man shuffles in a half circle and finds himself face-to-face with Liarbird.

'And who exactly are you, toots?'

Her stance is all attitude. 'Yeah, it's a good idea to keep calling me "toots" cause I won't hurt you much. I'm not Liarbird and I'm not pleased to meet you, you horrific and smelly old has-been.'

Mr Fabulous barks a sharp laugh that turns into a minor coughing fit. A couple of sparks of energy roll sluggishly across his back as he hacks. Finally he is able to say, 'Well, at least one of you is honest enough to say what she really thinks. Let's go and get something to eat. I've only had airline food for twenty-four hours. I'm starving.'

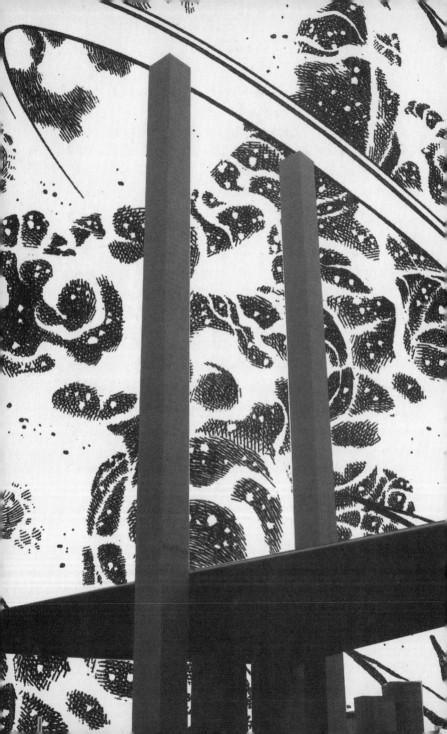

CHAPTER 20
LESS THAN FABULOUS

Laughter spills out from the porch where Mr Fabulous is playing cards and drinking whisky with Papa Torch and other long-lost Hero pals from the Golden Age. Old man laughter, in concert, as several old timers hack, wheeze and guffaw. On the lawn below the porch, the OK Team grumble.

'Is he here to train us or to get drunk?' hisses Yesterday.

'You should know,' says Cannonball nastily.

'Don't you start, brother dearest!'

'Start what? I'm too busy "visualising".'

Next to them, Torch sparks a flame onto his left index finger and gazes at it thoughtfully, as though he's never seen himself do his one trick before. I'm sitting cross-legged, frowning at my right hand, while Liarbird sits on the other side of the grass, muttering: 'Pink. Pink. Red. Rats! . . . Orange.'

Switchy is an anvil. He says he's 294 per cent sure that he's happy about that.

From the porch, another round of geriatric laughter can be heard.

'Ah Fab, that's a good one! You haven't changed a bit,' says a voice.

'Except for getting old,' Mr Fabulous replies.

'Yeah, well, you're not the Lone Ranger there.'

'The Lone Ranger!' says another old voice. 'Whatever happened to him?'

'Married his horse and moved to the suburbs is what I heard.'

Laughter peels off the porch one more time.

'Hey, Fab.' It's an impossibly tall man, slightly stooped by age but still scraping the roof. I wonder if he's related to Lurch?

'What, Mantis?'

'You won't believe who is still around, now posing as a respectable artist.'

'Um . . . Brown Nugget, the Human Poo? He was a nasty Villain.'

'No, but good try,' chuckles Mantis. 'I was talking about Scorch.'

Mr Fabulous is silent for a moment. 'Are you serious?'

'He's using the name "William Weld". Makes metal artwork with his power, melting metal together for rich idiots to blow their money on.'

'I can't believe he's allowed to roam free.'

'He did his time. Got parole ten years ago and took on the new name. What can anybody do?'

'Does he know I'm in town?'

'No idea. But watch your back. He still packs a punch.'

'Yeah, well, I ain't dead yet either. Whose deal is it? I wish the Ace was here. He'd be dealing ten hands a minute. And nothing but aces and kings.'

They all laugh.

I scowl up at the verandah. 'Man, this isn't what I expected at all.'

'Look, it's not my place to say, but he gave us instructions,' says Torch hesitantly. 'We have exercises to do.'

'Yeah, but shouldn't he be down here, teaching us and urging us on?'

Torch shrugs, not one for arguments. He lights his index finger for the hundredth time that hour and points it at a gum tree on the other side of the lawn. Nothing happens.

An hour or so ago, Mr Fabulous stood in the middle of the lawn with his wrinkly hands on his hips, the aged material of his costume hanging under what's left of his shrivelled biceps, and gave us a little speech.

'OK, you lot. The crooks aren't getting any weaker, they're getting tougher. So you need to get tougher too. Tougher and better, which is why we're going to get straight to it. You all have powers but they're undeveloped. It's time to train your skills, just like a tennis player has to work on his serve or a baseballer practises batting in the nets. Got it? Good.'

He wanders over to Cannonball. 'Show me what you do, helmet head.'

Cannonball poses in pre-flight mode. 'Let's fire the

cannon!' he yells confidently and zooms, a metre off the ground, straight backwards into a tree.

Mr Fabulous nods slowly. 'Right, lose the tag line, and focus on flying from where you are to the mailbox.'

'But that's only about two metres,' says Cannonball.

'Exactly. Small flights first . . . and like I said, lose the tag line. It's circa 1980.'

Cannonball hangs his head but nods.

Mr Fabulous's voice softens. 'More to the point, son, you're putting too much pressure on yourself by saying it. Golfers don't tell you which blade of grass they're going to land the ball on. They just concentrate on hitting the damn thing straight. All I'm saying is, fly first, then pose.'

Cannonball nods again. 'Thanks.'

Mr Fabulous turns to Yesterday. 'So, you can see into the past, huh? Well, as of now, we're working on making you see into the future. Watching your brother is as good as anything. Each time he aims for the mailbox, I want you to decide beforehand whether he's going to get there. Count how often you're right.'

'This shouldn't be hard.' Yesterday gives the old man a look, cocks her hip with arms folded, and watches her brother. He takes a deep breath and aims for the mailbox, eventually slamming into a car on the other side of the road.

'Hey, I was right! I thought he'd miss and he did. This is easy,' Yesterday grins.

'Yeah, well I'll only be impressed when you vote for him getting it right and he does,' Mr Fabulous says. 'Much longer odds. Who's next?'

Liarbird also has her arms folded across her chest, looking defiant. Mr Fabulous smiles. 'I like your spirit, kid. You're all right, even if your superpower makes me wonder whether you shouldn't be trying out as a super-villain. You don't want to lose your ability to lie convincingly. That's a handy skill to have if the team needs somebody to come up with a quick story under pressure. Hell, if your Hero career doesn't work out, you could be Prime Minister. But we need to get you telling fibs when you choose to, and that means being able to also tell the truth. Training ain't hard: just look at the sky and tell me what colour it is.'

Liarbird squints up at the cloudless sky and says, 'Green.'

Mr Fabulous smiles. 'What was that?'

'Red,' she says, frowning. 'Green! Yellow! Purple!'

'Keep at it,' he says, patting her shoulder. 'Focus. You told me that you become invisible when you're terrified, embarrassed or nervous. Is that right?'

'I told you that in confidence, yes,' I say through gritted teeth, feeling more than seeing Cannonball's smirk.

'Yeah, whatever. At least you don't wet your pants like some trainee Heroes, isn't that right, helmet head?'

'What? Hey!' says Cannonball.

'The point,' Mr Fabulous continues, 'is that your power's pretty good once you can control it. You *can* actually turn invisible, pass through walls, stuff like that. Not to be sneezed at. All we have to do is train you up so you choose when to do that stuff, and when to be solid. Let's start with something small. Try to turn your right hand invisible, but not the rest of your body. Just your hand.'

'I have no idea how,' I stammer, looking at my hand as though it is some kind of an alien creature – which, now I think about it, would be pretty cool as a Hero feature. Alien Hand!

'Just think about it,' Mr Fabulous says, bringing me back to the task. 'Pretend the hand is holding a rose for your girlfriend, Liarbird, over there and you don't want her to see it.'

I gulp and glance at Liarbird. Then I zap out of sight, before warping in and out of focus wildly. She is looking wide-eyed at me too, a look of astonishment on her reddening face.

'I didn't hear that,' she says. 'I didn't hear a thing.'

'Good,' I say, turning back to glare at our mentor.

He smiles broadly and gives me a wink, his eyes pure evil enjoyment. 'Even at my age, X-ray vision all but gone, super heat ray only luke warm, I can still see what I need to see.' He turns from me and looks around, at the trees, at the mailbox, at a garden gnome next to the porch stairs. 'Switchy, what or who are you at the moment?'

'I'm 900 per cent right here,' says Switchy in his gangly, acne-ridden teenage version, standing behind the ageing Hero.

'Oh, right. It's not exactly an improvement, is it? Well kid, your talent will take time to master but it's worth it, if we can get it right. The good news is that roughly three per cent of shape-shifters learn to control their skill and have Hero careers.'

'Three per cent!'

'Better odds than Heroes who can eat their own heads.'

'Euugh, really?' says Switchy.

154

'Training for you will be fun.' Mr Fabulous hands him a postcard. It is a signed autographed photograph of Mr Fabulous himself, circa 1940, in his youthful prime. His outfit shines, the golden F on his chest gleams and he is all muscle and attitude, soaring through clouds.

'I want you to turn into me, just like I used to be in this picture; not the broken down old geriatric standing in front of you now. Got it? Jeepers, if I could shape-shift back to my prime, you know I would, so try hard, son. I'm jealous.'

Switchy looks at the photo, concentrates hard, holds his breath, turns slightly pink and then POP!, just like that, he has changed into R2D2 from *Star Wars*.

'Bleet. Whistle! 400 per cent Whirr!' R2D2 says, rocking on his two legs. Then he turns pink and POP!, changes into a crayfish.

'This might take a while, Switchy. Keep at it. And don't wreck that photo in your pincers. I only brought a couple of dozen with me.'

Mr Fabulous gazes around at the various team members working on their skills. Cannonball misses the mailbox by a couple of metres. Yesterday frowns. Liarbird says 'Violet', and I'm still staring at my hand – making very sure I don't look at Liarbird.

'I don't want to get in the way, but what about me, Mr Fabulous?'

It is Torch, who has been standing quietly to the side, as is his style.

'Kid Torch! You've got to stop standing in the shadows if you want to be a Hero! Embrace the fact you're special, son. Live a little.'

Torch flicks his right index finger into flame. 'But that's it. That's all I've got.'

'Says you, kid. Trust me, I've known your grandpa how long? If you're a Torch then you've got more than that going for you. For starters, what happens when you shoot the flame?'

'Shoot the flame? I can't shoot the flame.'

'Can't? Or haven't tried?'

Torch opens his mouth, then closes it again.

'I thought so,' says Mr Fabulous. 'So we have a starting point. See that tree there, the big gum tree? Set fire to it, from over here. That's about six metres away. Point your finger and set the flame to fry.'

'But what happens if I actually manage to do it?'

'Um, the tree burns. Was that a trick question?'

'Is that all right, to burn a tree?'

Mr Fabulous chuckles. 'It won't burn for long. Aquagob is on the porch, waiting to play cards. Isn't that right, Aquagob?'

An old guy with wrinkles on wrinkles, dressed in a blue and green suit and gumboots, nods and then opens his mouth. But instead of saying 'That's right', he spits several litres of water across the porch, splashing Papa Torch from head to toe.

'Aquagob, you idiot!' Papa Torch fumes. He briefly flickers into pale flame, the fire spluttering but lasting long enough to burn off the water. 'Lucky you didn't hit Cardboard Man.'

'Yeah, you're telling me,' says an old Hero who appears to be made out of grocery boxes and shoe boxes. 'It reminds me of that time in 1954 when the swamp men of Snissangablaar managed to surround me with their watery ooze and –'

'Yeah, yeah, yeah. It took you three weeks in the sun to dry out. We know. We've only heard that story about 500 times,' says the Human Magpie.

'It's still a good story,' mumbles Cardboard Man.

'Ah, it's great to see you guys!' Mr Fabulous celebrates by flying into the air, doing a slow-motion, arthritic-looking somersault and then drifting unevenly onto the porch. As he lands, he's panting as though he's just run a marathon. 'I've said it before and I'll say it again, whose deal is it?'

157

THE TORCH

AGE: 13 years old
HERO GRADING: Entry Level, Grade 3
KNOWN POWERS: ▶ Ability to light flames on index fingers
KNOWN CATCHCRIES:
Doesn't say much.

CHAPTER 21
BACK TO REALITY

t school, I barely notice what class I'm in or what we are supposed to be learning. I spend the whole time staring at my hands, trying to make one of them lose focus while the rest of me stays solid – well, as solid as I ever am. After two days, I know deep down that it's never going to happen, but I keep at it, because our mentor has asked. I at least have to try, even if it's pointless.

One morning, at recess, I'm surprised to see Ali Fraudulent sitting on the far side of the school oval. She is lying on her back and staring at the sky. Strangest of all, it looks as though the girl who never speaks is moving her mouth, murmuring something to herself and frowning. I've never heard her even attempting to talk – I didn't know she was capable of speech – and I wish I could hear what she is saying. Frederick Fodder and Simon Fondue walk past, huddled in their own secret world. They are looking closely at Simon's left hand.

Then Frederick's little sister walks past, sees me and winks.

How strange, I think, but then remember what I'm supposed to be doing. I gaze again at my right hand, which steadfastly refuses to become any more or less out of focus than the rest of me.

Gee, that's a surprise.

At lunchtime, I head to the library, as usual, and bump into Simon Fondue and Frederick Fodder. As I walk past, Simon says, 'Hey Hazy, when do we get to start making "one arm bandit" jokes?'

'What?' I ask. 'I'm not a poker machine.'

'No,' he says, with a secretive smile. 'But you're not Two-gun Pete, either . . . all going well.'

He and Frederick grin at me like idiots, like I'm missing some great joke, but I'm mystified, so I keep moving. A couple of desks on, my heart jumps because I see the white hair of Ali Fraudulent bent over a book called *Lies and Truth*.

I'm too worn out from practising to bother feeling nervous, so I walk straight up and ask, 'Excuse me, Ali?'

She looks at me with those grey eyes of hers and I feel myself becoming instantly fuzzy. But she looks welcoming and starts to smile.

'Um, is anybody sitting here?' I manage, pointing to the chair across from her.

She nods enthusiastically, still smiling.

'So it's taken? I can't join you?'

She shakes her head.

'Oh,' I say in disappointment. 'Oh well, never mind.'

I turn to go and am shocked to hear her voice, for the first time ever.

She says simply: 'Go.'

'Fine, I will,' I say. 'I'm going. Jeez.'

The weird thing is that her voice sounds strangely familiar. I wander over to the other side of the library, looking for somewhere else to sit. The only place is near Frederick's sister.

I sit down and little Alexandra Fodder says, 'I knew you were going to sit there.'

'Good for you,' I say, and open my book.

CHAPTER 22

ENOUGH IS ENOUGH

*W*e practise for a couple of weeks. There's no point going through it blow by blow. Every day is pretty much the same. We run through the practice drills Mr Fabulous has set for us, while he plays cards with his old-time mates. We get frustrated and go nowhere. He tells us to keep going. We show zero improvement.

'When you want to get somewhere, you'll get somewhere,' he says.

'What do you mean?' Cannonball almost screams. 'We're working our butts off here and nothing's happening.'

'It takes more than work.'

'What does that mean?'

Mr Fabulous just smiles mysteriously. I go back to staring at my hand and wondering why it won't disappear. Liarbird looks up, muttering, 'Green, green, green.' Yesterday says,

'Anywhere but the tree,' and Cannonball flies anywhere but at the tree. Switchy shifts randomly from a bowling ball to a lighthouse, to his own Hero form – but not Mr Fabulous – to a giraffe to a cool car. There's no pattern to his shape-shifting and the occasional rude word. Torch just stares sadly at the candle on the end of his finger, with the occasional sheepish glance towards the porch, where Old Man Torch, the most famous of the Torches, deals another hand.

It's as if the OK Team is caught in an endless night.

Until one day, Torch swears the flame on his finger actually reaches about ten centimetres towards the tree. He tries to do it again but it won't work while we're all watching.

Then Cannonball slams into the letterbox. Even his bravado can't convince us he actually controlled the flight but, even if it was random chance, he definitely went where he was supposed to fly. He misses the next thirty attempts. But it's something. Suddenly he can see a future.

Which is a lot more than I can, staring at my stubbornly visible right hand.

I realise I'm close to wanting to punch Cannonball. Yes, he may be my original Hero partner and he may have saved my life in that alley, but if he keeps strutting around like God's gift to Heroes, frowning at how crap the rest of the team is, while he still can't actually fly straight, apart from that once, I'm going to attack him with a rake or something.

Another day, I'm sitting next to Switchy and he changes from a toy robot into his muscle-bound genuine Hero form, and then into his gangly, pimple-faced self, and slumps on the grass.

'Switchy, can I ask you something personal?' I say.

'I guess.'

'When you change back into yourself, like now, why don't you try to use your power to get rid of the acne?'

Switchy looks embarrassed.

'Hey Switchy,' I press on. 'It's not like we haven't all got zits here and there. But you could get rid of yours.'

He plucks some blades of grass then looks at me with a strange intensity. 'The thing is, Focus, I don't think that this –' he waves a hand from his face to his feet – 'is actually me.'

'It's not?'

'No more than the small dog, the toy robot or the heroic Hero persona. The truth is, I feel like I'm eighty-seven per cent sure that I'm playing a role in this body, just like the others.'

'There must be times when you relax, when you really relax. What are you then?'

'That's the thing, Focus. When I'm asleep, I'm a pillow or a sleeping bag, or maybe Sleeping Beauty. The rest of the time, I switch. Honestly, I don't think I know who I really am.'

'Wow,' I say. 'Is that why you always talk about being 400 per cent sure about stuff? Because you're not sure about anything?'

'I guess,' he says.

'That's heavy.'

Sometimes I catch Liarbird looking at me, or she catches me looking at her, and we both quickly look away. One day she says to me, 'Girls who want to drink hot chocolates with boys in Belgium often stand on their heads for more than nine hours before attempting sudoku puzzles.'

If you understand girls and can help me work this one out, you're a greater Hero than the whole team put together. Sometimes talking to her is like speaking with a Crypto Twin.

Finally, late one afternoon, Mr Fabulous steps off the porch, watches us all for a while and sighs. 'It's not working,' he says. 'Time for Plan B.'

'What's Plan B?' asks Yesterday nervously.

'It's simpler than this one. We boot you in the deep end with some bad guys and you either swim or you drown.'

'Gee, that's a top idea,' says Liarbird.

'Hey, toots, you think I want to spend a year here, watching you get the sky colour wrong? I'm not getting any younger, in case you hadn't noticed. I've only got so many days left on this Earth, capeesh?'

'Capeesh?' asks Torch.

'It means "understand". You should watch more television. Hey, fuzzy-wuzzy freak show, have you made your hand vanish yet?'

'No,' I say, thinking Mr Fabulous almost matches Scumm for rudeness.

'Good,' Mr Fabulous says. 'Then you can use both hands to bring me two beers.'

We break for dinner, supplied by Mrs Torch. I phone home and tell my mum that I'm staying at a school friend's house to finish some homework.

'It's lovely you're finally making some friends, Hazy,' says Mum.

'Isn't it,' I reply.

'Is this a boy your father and I would like?'

I watch Torch lighting candles on the dining room table with the flame from his hand.

'Yeah, I guess. Dad sure would,' I say. 'A whole new person to tell "interesting facts" to.'

After dinner, Mr Fabulous stands, stretches, claps his hands and leads us back onto the front lawn.

'Right,' he says. 'Let's go find us some bad guys.'

Cannonball puffs out his chest and asks, 'You think we're as ready as the sun at dawn, huh?'

'Not really, but I want to get home to Gotham before 2047. You've gotta get your butts kicked some time, so why not now?'

'It's the unwavering belief that I love,' Yesterday says out of the side of her mouth.

'I've heard there's a new band of teenagers riding their skateboards in the private car park of the dentist up on Grange Road,' says Torch.

Mr Fabulous is shaking his head. 'Kid, I love you, you know that. I love your family and I love your grandad. But you do not become a Hero to sort out skateboarding young punks on private property. You become a Hero to beat up super-villains. We're going to the city.'

'The city?' says Switchy, currently a mermaid.

'Yeah, big place with lots of tall buildings. Not far from here.'

'Are you planning to jump one?' says Cannonball.

'What?'

'A tall building. You could leap one, you know, in a single bound.'

'Maybe twenty years ago, kid. Now I'm happy to drink a coffee while you punks do the hard work. Come on, let's go.'

'I'm sorry to be speaking out of turn and all, but isn't the city centre where the big gangs hang out?' Torch persists.

'What?' says Mr Fabulous. 'You want to fight eight-year-old disgruntled boy scouts all your life?'

'I think eight year olds are more likely to be cubs,' Switchy points out, currently in the gangly pimply mode that may or may not be the real him. 'I'm 140 per cent certain you can't be a scout until you're older.'

Mr Fabulous is looking at him as though he is trying to remember how to use his heat ray to melt something. 'That wasn't my major point there, changey-boy.'

'Oh,' says Switchy, turning into a bag of cement.

'But Mr Fabulous . . . are we ready for the city?' Yesterday asks. 'Actually, I think I know the answer to that already.'

'The only way to become top level Heroes is to start punching above your weight. Don't believe all this crap about entry level this and grade that. See a bad guy. Beat him. It's that simple. You think I got to be who I am by hassling jay-walkers?'

'I'm not ready,' admits Torch.

'If I say you're ready then you're ready, Junior Flame. Let's go.'

'Mr Fabulous?' I'm the leader. I have to say something. 'Can we at least vote on whether we feel equipped to face a gang if and when we meet one in the city?'

The ageing Hero squints, looks at the sky, and thinks about it. 'No,' he says.

'This will go well,' says Liarbird as we head for the train station. 'Heroes who fail in their first attempt at fighting city bad guys get locked in a vault in Gotham and have lipstick painted on their noses.'

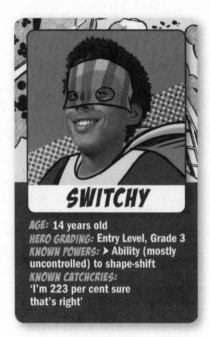

SWITCHY

AGE: 14 years old
HERO GRADING: Entry Level, Grade 3
KNOWN POWERS: ▶ Ability (mostly uncontrolled) to shape-shift
KNOWN CATCHCRIES:
'I'm 223 per cent sure that's right'

CHAPTER 23

THE BATTLE OF THE TICK TOCKS

We walk up and down the city's streets for forty minutes. Mr Fabulous looks mainly to the sky, between the tall buildings, before finally grinning and saying, 'What time is it?'

'Clobbering time?' says Cannonball hopefully.

'Maybe, son, maybe. Is it 8 pm?'

'No, it's 1 am,' says Liarbird.

'Huh?' says the old man.

'Actually it's 7 pm,' says Torch.

'I thought so.' Mr Fabulous starts for the building. 'All right, you lot. Onto the roof. Good luck.'

'Who are we fighting?' Yesterday wants to know.

'Who cares? Let's go get 'em like kangaroos in a supermarket,' says Cannonball.

'I'm not going up there until I know who I'm dealing with.'

Mr Fabulous looks at me and shakes his head slowly. 'You are a problem, son, but I'll humour you. It's Time-Zone. He's a low level villain who goes around changing clocks in public places. Likes to cause havoc with train timetables, things like that. He's tinkered with the Flinders Street clock, added an hour, contravening daylight saving adjustments.'

We look at one another. Torch shrugs.

'OK, let's go,' I say.

'Well, thank you,' Mr Fabulous says, dripping sarcasm. 'I'm honoured that the great Focus has seen fit to agree with my judgement.'

I can't help myself asking, 'Were you this crabby when you were in your prime?'

I'm expecting him to be mad, but instead he barks with laughter. 'At least twice as bad tempered. I've mellowed.'

'Gee, wish I'd known you then,' Liarbird mutters.

Yesterday looks nervous. 'What happens if they start winning?'

Mr Fabulous shrugs. 'Then you've got me. I mean, what am I? A block of flats?'

'Actually, sir, that's Switchy,' says Cannonball, standing beside a large apartment building that wasn't there a few moments ago.

'Oh, right. Nice switch, Switchy.' Mr Fabulous chuckles and shakes his head. 'You crazy kids.'

We take a lift to the fifteenth floor, emerging to find two doors. One is locked, chained and barred. The other is open and with a sign that reads 'Roof' with an arrow.

'This way!' says Cannonball.

'You're a genius,' Mr Fabulous sneers. 'Right, into formation please.'

'Guys, huddle!' I say. We come together, gloves touching in the middle as we've practised. Cannonball, Torch, Liarbird, Yesterday, Switchy and me. Mr Fabulous mutters and shakes his head in the background instead of joining in.

I look at my teammates' faces. They are white, sweating, scared. We're a long way from the ground, about to face a city villain.

'I'm OK!' I yell.

'You're OK!' they yell back.

'We're OK!' we finish together.

'Gee, why don't you make some more noise?' our mentor asks.

I can feel my focus wavering wildly, but tell myself it is excitement as well as fear. 'Let's go!' I say, and we burst through the door and up the stairs to the roof.

TimeZone is wearing huge black boots, watches up and down both arms, and a black skin-tight costume with a giant clockface on the front. I look closely and notice the clock's hour and minute hands are swinging wildly.

'Wow, how does he do that on his chest?' Torch asks.

'No idea, it must be some kind of battery,' says Switchy.

'Looks cool though,' I admit.

'We here for a fashion show or a fight?' Cannonball asks, storming past.

TimeZone yells, and suddenly five other villains appear from behind a massive metallic air conditioning unit. They are shorter but musclebound and wearing different-coloured costumes, the fronts of which are decorated with different clocks.

'It's the Tick Tocks, TimeZone's notorious henchmen!' yells Mr Fabulous. 'Designer Watch, Alarm Clock, Stop Watch, and the veteran henchmen, Grandfather Clock and Fobwatch!'

We fan out and I realise we are already down a member. I look wildly around and see Yesterday huddled against the air conditioning unit.

'Yesterday, what's wrong?'

'I'm scared of heights. It's so far down.'

'Stay there unless we need you,' I say. 'Switchy, can you turn into a giant clock?'

'I'll try,' he says and changes into a penguin. It shakes and turns red then tranforms into a giant glass of water. And finally a DVD player. At least it has a digital clock on the front.

'Ooh!' says TimeZone, waving his arms. 'Look, the time is correct on that DVD player. This won't do at all! Tick Tocks, go to work.'

They charge at Switchy, crawling all over him.

'How do you change the time on this thing?' asks Stop Watch.

'Is there a remote control?' Grandfather Clock frowns.

'Maybe there's an instruction manual,' suggests Fobwatch.

'Go,' I yell, and we charge. Cannonball isn't trying to fly so he actually makes it to them, swinging a huge punch that catches Designer Watch on the side of the head and sends him spinning to the other side of the roof.

Torch has his finger alight and is waving it in front of Alarm Clock, who looks more confused than scared.

Liarbird crouches down beside Fobwatch and says, 'If you press that button, it will change the clock.'

He presses the button and Switchy's disc eject knocks him – POW! – clean across the roof.

'Nice one, Liarbird,' I say, grinning, and turn my attention to TimeZone himself. It occurs to me that the OK Team is almost winning. Our first battle against a genuine villain, with henchmen and everything, and we are doing pretty well. The very thought of it is so satisfying I feel my body become more or less solid, and that's when TimeZone punches me.

I have never been hit so hard. It's like being hit by a sledgehammer and my whole stomach feels like it's turned inside out. The force of the blow lifts me into the air and to the very edge of the roof. I sway for a moment, trying to get my balance, still in shock from being actually punched.

'Cannonball!' yells Liarbird, looking at me in horror, and I just have time to think stupidly that it's cool she obviously cares before I topple off the side.

The fall is unimaginably far. Fifteen storeys is a long way down, I think, as I plummet towards the road, far below. Of course, the fright sends my entire body completely out of whack to the point that I am invisible, and I feel myself slow in the air as my body mass disappears. Now I'm floating – a bunch of disconnected atoms drifting through space – and it occurs to me that if I could stay like that, I wouldn't actually hit the ground. In fact, if I could do this deliberately, I could fly.

The thought of choosing to fly is so empowering that I become solid again and fall fast. There are now about nine storeys between me and the hard tarmac and concrete below. And that's when Switchy falls past me. I find out later that Grandfather Clock and Fobwatch got tired of trying to change his DVD clock display and instead attacked him with pieces of timber. Switchy managed to change into his Genuine Hero form, which had them cowering, but then accidentally switched again, into a small duck. They lunged at him and, in trying to get out of their way, he fell off the roof.

As he falls past me, he begins to switch desperately, but only manages to turn into a piano, then a bowling ball, and then a giant hammer. By the time he hits the footpath, he is an anvil, like in the cartoons, and leaves a hole where he lands. Ouch.

Of course, that is enough to freak me right out and, with one storey to go and falling unimaginably fast, my body whacks out again. I fall straight *through* the ground, somehow passing through concrete and pipes and tiling before landing heavily on the platform of an underground train station.

Dazed and confused, I stagger to a bench and sit for a few seconds. Then I walk over to the turnstiles leading to the escalators and to street level. A railway official looks suspiciously at my silver cargo pants, T-shirt and, most of all, my cape, eyes narrowing.

'Where's your ticket, son?' he asks.

'I didn't catch the train,' I say. 'I, um, just fell into the station.'

'Of course you did. Young punks, think you can ride for free around the city. Do you have a ticket or not?'

'I didn't catch the train,' I repeat.

He pulls an official-looking book out of his back pocket. 'The fine for riding without the correct fare is one hundred dollars, kid. There goes your pocket money.'

CHAPTER 24
EXILE

I find the team down an alley, slumped in groups.

'All you had to do was stay a duck,' Mr Fabulous is ranting to Switchy, who sports a large white bandage around his head and looks a little glassy-eyed. 'Ducks can fly, you idiot. Why couldn't you stay a duck?'

He turns on Yesterday. 'Afraid of heights? How can a superhero be afraid of heights? And why didn't you foresee that it would be a problem, psychic girl? You were pathetic!'

Yesterday starts to cry, but he has already moved on to Liarbird.

'Nice move with the DVD eject, but other than that, you were hopeless, Liarbird. You've got to learn to throw a punch. That's the most honest thing there is. A knuckle sandwich!'

'I'm heavyweight champion of the world,' she says miserably.

Cannonball is standing to one side. 'How'd I go, coach? Was I better than a sandwich in a toaster?'

'You weren't bad, Cannonball,' Mr Fabulous admits, patting Cannonball on the back. 'Sure, it was a lucky break when you tried to fly straight at Alarm Clock and accidentally took out TimeZone instead, but I guess that was the point of the exercise.'

Torch is hanging his head, unable to look anybody in the eye. 'I was crap, wasn't I, sir?'

'You'll get better, Torch. Hang in there, kid.'

Torch shuffles his feet. 'It was an honour to see you in action, sir. You took out all five Tick Tocks.'

'Just like the old days. I've still got it every now and then.' Mr Fabulous stands a little taller than usual. Then he sees me.

'Look everybody, the fearless leader returns! And where exactly have you been?'

'I fell into the underground station,' I say, and they all stare. As proof, I hold up a slip of paper. 'I got fined for not having the correct ticket.'

I catch Cannonball's eye and he starts to laugh.

Torch and Yesterday start to laugh as well. Even Switchy, looking groggy, manages a grin.

Mr Fabulous opens and closes his mouth and finally just shakes his head in disbelief.

Only Liarbird isn't laughing. As the others are doubled over in hysterics, she comes over and unexpectedly wraps her arms around me. Squeezing tightly, she says softly,

'I wasn't worried. I didn't think you were dead.'

Then she lets me go, looking embarrassed.

I turn my back on everyone and adjust my silver shoe, blushing furiously. But I'm also humiliated that the rest of the team laughed at me. I've let them all down.

I feel Mr Fabulous's eyes on me. Maybe it's the remnants of his X-ray vision?

'Hey kid,' he says.

'It's Focus, Mr Fabulous.' Even I hear the edge in my voice.

'Sir,' he says.

'There's no need to call me "sir",' I reply. 'Focus is fine.' Yes, I'm in a mood. So sue me.

He looks at me for the longest time. 'I wasn't calling you "sir", you moron. I was saying that you should call me "sir".'

'Oh really?,' I say.

'Yes, really. And it's: Really, sir.'

I don't know where this is going. In fact, I feel like I'm walking on a thin roof, so I need to tread warily. I quietly turn away.

'Hey kid.'

He is still talking to me.

'Yes, Mr Fabulous? Sir?'

He seems to miss the sarcasm. 'Clean my cape.'

'What?'

'Are you deaf as well as stupid? I said clean my cape. It got grease spilt on it during the battle with the Tick Tocks.'

I can't help myself. I'm furious. 'I didn't become a superhero to clean people's capes.'

'Well, I didn't come all the way to Australia to listen to hissy fits from a human cloud. You want to be in this team, learn some humility. The only thing super about you, kid, is the size of your ego.'

'Mr Fabulous!'

'Sir.'

I try to take a deep breath. I'm suddenly aware of the rest of the team watching this exchange, open-mouthed, like it is a tennis match between a penguin and a ghost. Or something unusual. You know.

Me? I'm trying hard not to cry. That would be very un-super.

'Mr Fabulous, sir . . . all I'm trying to do is improve. For example, I'd like to talk to you about leadership. I know you weren't ever part of a team, apart from occasionally helping out the Really Heroic Heroes of America, but I'd love to hear your thoughts on how I could be better at —'

He waves a gloved hand in dismissal. 'You're no longer leading the team, son. Torch is.'

'Excuse me?'

'Torch?' says Cannonball, before a glare from Mr Fabulous shuts him up.

I see spots. 'But what do you mean? I'm the leader. This is my team!'

'Not any more. The way I see it, if you really believe in the team, then you'll be happy to play the best role you can for that team, and that's not leader.'

'Says who?'

'Says me, kid.' His voice rises dangerously. 'The guy who's in the Hall of Fame and has flown halfway around the world to lick you bums into shape. I don't think it's healthy for this team to have a guy who can't even keep himself in focus as their leader. Have you thought about the symbolism of that? The fact that every time you go into battle, your sterling leadership is to practically disappear as soon as somebody looks like throwing a punch? Torch is the new boss.'

'But . . .' is all I can manage. My world is caving in.

Unbelievably, Mr Fabulous starts chuckling. 'You'll find this funny, kid. I would have made Liarbird leader except she would have pointed everybody in the wrong direction all the time. Isn't that funny? Switchy could have led too, except that you'd all have trouble taking orders from a waste-paper basket. What a crack-up. Isn't that a crack-up?'

I'm so upset I'm practically invisible.

(183)

'Ah, take it on the chin, will ya, kid? You're supposed to be a Hero, not a cry-baby. You're still in the team, and you'll improve if you keep listening to me. So no whingeing. Torch deserves your support.'

'Have you made him leader because you are mates with his grandfather?'

It's out before I even realise I'm going to say it. Mr Fabulous stops in his tracks and gives me a hard look that would halt an army from the planet Tarantulum. And those guys are said to be tough.

'How dare you, kid. Pull yourself together, no pun intended. Clearly your ego can't handle being part of the team instead of the headliner in your own little world, so here's the latest news: take a hike. There must be some fresh talent in this crappy town to replace you. I met a dead kid the other day who was keen to join up, so you can consider yourself replaced.'

'You met Super Dead Kid?'

'I dunno if he was super, but he sure was dead. Kept telling me how long he'd been forced to walk the Earth.'

'Yeah, that's him,' I say miserably.

'Swell. Thanks for coming, Focus. Have a great life. All right, those who do want to be in the team, let's head back to base, do some stretches and debrief. Good job.'

I blink. My lip trembles. I'm definitely crying now. Luckily I think I am so far out of whack, visually, that nobody would know that tears are running down my cheeks. I'm humiliated, angry, shocked and stunned, all at the same time.

I am vaguely aware of the looks the rest of the team are giving me as they slink off after the old man in the faded yellow cape. I am determined not to look at Liarbird because if she seems sympathetic, I'll howl. I look at Switchy instead, but it's hard to see his expression because he is in the shape of a motorised golf buggy. Cannonball tries to give me a smile but it looks more like a grimace. Torch looks at Mr Fabulous walking away, looks at me, and then shrugs helplessly, in an 'I have nothing to do with this' sort of way.

I just wave Torch away. I don't want to talk to anybody.

As they leave, I hear Yesterday saying to Mr Fabulous, 'I knew you were going to do that.'

And then they walk around the corner and they are gone.

I'm a thirteen-year-old kid wearing spray-painted silver cargo pants, a silver T-shirt, a home-made cape and silver gloves. I'm a long way from home and I'm crying my eyes out. I'm all alone.

I don't feel very super.

YESTERDAY

AGE: 11 years old
HERO GRADING: Not graded
KNOWN POWERS:
➤ Claims to have the ability to 'see into the past'
KNOWN CATCHCRIES:
'I knew you were going to say that'

ANCHOR: You're watching Channel 78737 – where every day is more super than the last. Hey, here's a surprise. A Hero Association Hall of Famer has turned up in Australia, of all places. Yes, Golden Age star Mr Fabulous seems to have emerged from retirement to test what must be fading powers against some B and C grade villains.

Why? Well, the man himself says he is purely active as a super coach these days, but sometimes at the coalface, he's been forced to help out.

Mr Fabulous is on screen, with a microphone in front of him. In the background, Torch is hiding his face behind his long hair while Cannonball walks through the back of shot, once, then twice, and a third time, trying to look as though he has no idea the camera is there.

MR FABULOUS: I'm over here as a favour to an old buddy who used to fire up the Hero world, if that rings any bells. I'm working with a bunch of kid Heroes, and they're good kids but raw. They had a little trouble finding their focus, but now they're on the right track. The problem with this job is that you can only be in a training situation for so long, then you have to meet the bad guys face-to-face. A couple of times I've needed to step in, to ensure the right side won.

SUPER REPORTER: How do your powers hold up now, Mr Fabulous?

MR FABULOUS: Well, let's just say I wouldn't want to be taking on Fangular9 or the Evil Nasty Gang in their prime right now. My super heat-ray is only lukewarm these days, so I think I might leave the higher-grade villains to Golden Boy or any other Triple As who live around here.

SUPER REPORTER: Then again, Golden Boy has not actually recorded a single-handed world save at this stage of his career. Australia might need somebody with your record after all.

MR FABULOUS: Don't you worry about Golden Boy. He just needs to find himself at home plate when it matters. He knows how to swing the bat.

(SILENCE)

MR FABULOUS: That was a baseball analogy.

CHAPTER 25
A MYSTERIOUS PARCEL

Somehow, having not slept at all, I make it through the next day at school. When I get back home, I trudge literally through the front door of our house, too preoccupied to realise the door isn't open.

'Hello, Hazy darling,' says my mum. 'Please try not to walk through the door. You know it upsets the neighbours.'

'Sorry, Mum,' I say absently. 'I'm heading up to my room.'

'Again? You never seem to come out of that cave any more, Hazy.'

I don't answer. I just walk up the stairs, fall on the bed and turn on the TV.

I switch to Channel 78737. Hero after hero has been pulling off astonishing rescues. There's a major report about a giant meteor on a collision course with Australia but it's assumed that one of the Triple A Heroes will deal with it – maybe even Golden Boy for his long-awaited first world save. Everything is running smoothly in the Hero World. And it occurs to me that I'm the one who doesn't fit in.

I lie on my bed and find myself looking at the poster of the actor playing the Southern Cross, and remember the moment I realised Leon was standing there and I was talking to a Hero. I remember the feeling of being told I had a superpower too.

What if Leon got it wrong?

What if I've got it completely wrong?

What if there is no place in the Hero line-up for some kid who doesn't know if he's even got a body at any given moment?

Who am I kidding?

There's a knock on the door.

'Hazy, dear? You received a package today.'

'I did?' I get up off the bed as Mum comes in with a cardboard parcel about the size of a small shoebox.

'Have you ordered any books on eBay or Amazon?'

'No.' I bend my head and listen to the parcel, but it is silent.

'Honestly, Hazy Retina,' Mum says. 'You think somebody would have a reason to send a bomb to a thirteen-year-old boy?'

'Can't be too careful, Mum,' I say, wishing I could tell her I'm only following correct Hero procedure, as outlined in the Hero guidebook's regulations regarding receipt of anonymous mail.

Of course, the package is addressed to 'Hazy Retina',

so there's no reason to think it has anything to do with my Hero double-life. But somehow I know better. I take the package and shoo Mum out of my room.

The back of the wrapping gives me no clues. The 'sender' box is blank, which is really strange. If the package had come from the Australian Federation of Hero Types, they would have used the accepted coded address with the fictitious suburb 'Upper Lower Gotham Heights'. I take a deep breath, tear into the cardboard wrapper and find a box. Inside the box is a single DVD. Somebody has written in felt-tip pen on the DVD: 'Focus'.

My heart begins to thump. Somebody knows my secret identity.

I look again at the wrapping, this time at the front, and gasp. The stamps are from the USA. A smudged stamp says 'New York', with a picture of an American flag.

Head spinning – but not literally – I carefully pick up the silver disc. My fingers are such a blur with nerves that I can hardly hold it. Finally I manage to insert the DVD in the drive and sit back while it loads.

Finally the image of a man's head appears on screen, but something must be wrong with the disc because the image is broken up into tiny blocks, as though it has been computer-distorted. I'm crushed with disappointment. But then I look more carefully at the image and I realise that the background is crystal clear. Massive skyscrapers are visible out the window. It is only the man's head that is distorted.

I'm looking at my Uncle Blinky!

I hit 'play'.

'Hazy Retina!' he says. 'I hear you're pretty smart, so you've probably worked out who I am. Hiya kid. How ya doin'?'

My uncle has obviously been in the USA long enough to pick up a strong accent.

'I was gonna drop you an email, kid, but whaddaya gonna do? I'm always a little concerned about security,' Blinky says from the DVD. 'I thought a little face-to-face time, blur-to-blur, would be better. (That blur-to-blur thing was a little joke, kid. You gotta have a sense of humour when you look like me. Or you. Right? Of course, I'm right.)

'I gotta tell you, Hazy, life is pretty damn sweet over here. Court TV does nuthin but show the legal system, for all its sins, and I got more work comin' in than you could poke a bagel at. You know what I'm sayin'?'

'Anyways, what I wanted to tell you is that I've been following your little adventures from over here. I kinda like your team's costumes – a little "ghetto fabulous" maybe, but they're fun.'

'*Ghetto fabulous?*' I think, storing that term away for later research.

'That means, like, a little too flashy,' says the video image of my uncle, as though reading my mind. 'A little too on the side of razzle-dazzle, even for New Yorkers.'

I'm suddenly glad I didn't go with tassles on my cape.

Uncle Blinky is still talking. 'I know it will surprise you that I can know about your little OK thingo from this far away but, trust me, the Hero world is smaller than it looks. Let's just say I gotta few friends in Gotham and they keep me up to date with what I need to know. Occasionally we go to a ball game or maybe catch a show on Broadway if one of 'em's in town, and they might mention that you've had your butt kicked from Melbourne to Chicago one more time.'

Briefly, I'd been trying to picture a bunch of superheroes watching a Broadway musical, but now my shoulders slump at my uncle's off-hand dismissal of the OK Team's dismal efforts.

'Kid, don't worry about it,' Blinky says. The pixels move and I think he's smiling. 'Holey schamoley, you gotta start somewhere! So don't give in, that's all I'm sayin'. Stare down the doubters. Be The Man. You are a Hero, and that's all that counts. Never, ever forget the all important motto, kiddo: 'A Hero is a Hero. No matter what. You've just gotta believe.'

'Got that? Ok, later, dude. See ya.'

Something blurry that is probably Blinky's hand looms in front of the picture and then the screen goes black.

I watch the entire video five more times. Something is lurking at the edge of my brain, but it's like when I turn my internal eye to it, it scuttles off into the shadows. I close my eyes, take a deep breath. Picture Uncle Blinky in his self-confident, glorious blurriness.

A Hero is a Hero. No matter what.

I'm OK. You're OK.

Leon flying in my room.

The Victorian Society for the Blurred.

You are a Hero! Leon saying that. Uncle Blinky saying that.

I am a Hero.

193

Mr Fabulous saying I'm not.

A Hero is a Hero. No matter what.

Mr Fabulous firing me from MY team. Mr blow-in-from-nowhere, fancy-Hall-of-Fame crapulous.

A Hero is a Hero. Me.

By now I'm steamed. 'I AM A HERO!' I yell. I jump around the room, getting madder and madder. 'I AM A HERO!'

Suddenly I catch sight of myself in the mirror. By rights, I should be invisible, I'm so worked up, but instead, I look in the mirror and I can see . . . me! Crystal clear and razor sharp! Scowling and with eyes that burn. How strange that I am so *in* focus. If only I could be like this *and* be out of whack, when I chose instead of at random.

I'll do it, I think to myself. The old man can go eat his cape. I WILL be a Hero. I WILL learn to control my power and I WILL make a difference. I will be more fabulous than Mr Fabulous ever was.

What was the old bighead's training regime? Make my hand vanish when the rest of me is visible? Sure. I can do that because at this moment, I decide I can. I'm not some loser ex-leader. I'm not some wannabe Hero.

I am a Hero.

A Hero is a Hero. No matter what.

I'm not even Hazy Retina at this moment. He doesn't exist.

I am Focus.

And then I look at my right arm and I almost have a heart attack. You won't believe it, but yes, my hand is gone. No hand. Tentatively, I reach for a pen on the table next to the mirror with the invisible hand. I pick it up and watch the pen float by itself through the air. Too cool!

I take the pen in my left hand and wave my right hand in front of it. The pen disappears as my invisible hand covers it.

This is too much. I feel excitement rising and I drop the pen without letting go of it. I look in the mirror. Without me realising, excitement has made my entire body become a smudge. Rats.

But for a moment . . . for one moment, I did it.

It can be done.

CHAPTER 26
THE END OF THE WORLD?

Over the next week, I practise every chance I get. At school I stay away from the library, sneaking to a quiet place behind a tree at the back of the football oval to stare at my hand. I try not to think about it, then think about it hard for a few seconds, and sometimes I am sure it becomes more blurry than the rest of me. A lot of the time I can't be certain. Once or twice, I definitely nail it. In the privacy of my room, I even try willing my head to disappear instead of my hand. If nothing else, it would make a great party trick.

All week, I don't see any more reports about the OK Team or Mr self-promoter Fabulous. To be honest, I don't turn on Channel 78737 much, just in case the team does turn up – group hugging, saving the world, and doing interviews about how great life is without their loser of a former leader.

Of course, I have some all-new pressing problems of my own. Am I going to stay a Hero? Should I attempt to join another team? Or try going solo? What can I actually achieve on my own?

The worst thing is that I feel so alone. At the end of the day, the OK Team had been my best, maybe only friends. I even miss Torch, now leader of the pack and destined for Hero greatness as I choke on his fiery dust. As for Liarbird, you can take a guess.

I imagine bumping into her in the street, or unexpectedly on a super job.

'Do you miss me?' I'd ask.

'You bet,' she'd say. 'More than I could ever have imagined. My life is incomplete.'

Then I'd remember her power and sag.

The only good thing is that Boris Scumm seems to have lost interest in me. Twice I turn a corner to find myself face-to-blurry-face with him and his gang but, apart from a cruel sneer and a few stray insults, they leave me alone. Scumm and his chief henchmen are in huddles a lot lately, talking excitedly and sneaking glances over their shoulders. They are clearly up to no good, but as long as it doesn't involve me, I'm happy.

Nine days after I fall out of the OK Team, I receive an All Points Bulletin email from the Hero Association, asking all local heroes to a briefing regarding a Category Three Star threat. Looking up the Hero handbook, I discover that Category Three Star means 'Earth-threatening', even higher in danger than Category Nine Radiation. The meeting is to be held at the old Spencer Street power plant, the venue for Heroes Anonymous, where I met Cannonball all that time ago.

I decide to turn up. Not that I'm likely to have anything to do with a Category Three Star threat, but I might be able to meet some new Heroes, ask if there are any teams starting up.

I tell Mum and Dad that I'm going to play Warhammer at Games Workshop in the city.

'I still don't understand why you always wear that silver outfit to play a board game,' Mum says.

'It's just part of the fun,' I reply. 'Helps get my imagination flowing.'

'What does the big F stand for?'

'Um, "fun".'

She looks unconvinced. 'So, do you wear a giant H when you do your homework?'

'It's good he's making friends, Iris. Let him go,' says Dad. 'Hazy, did you know that a guy called Tom on myspace.com is on record as having the most friends of anybody in the world, with more than sixty million friends?'

'That must cost a lot in birthday cards,' I say. Dad starts laughing, so I run before he can think of any more freak yarns.

At the power plant, I have my usual moment of wondering how I'm going to get through or over the massive brick wall, but then I think for a second that I see Switchy and Yesterday entering the alley and I blur out of focus so fast that it's nothing to slip straight through the bricks.

There are dozens of Heroes present. I find a seat down the back, next to a guy who looks to be dressed as a pumpkin.

Next to him is a girl with hundreds of surfboard legropes hanging off her costume. I don't dare even ask . . .

I'm stunned but satisfied to spy Lurch way over the other side of the room. So he *is* a Hero. And he's sitting next to Old Man Mantis. I always knew.

Because this is a Hero gathering, there is no need for a temporary stage. Instead, the Southern Cross floats off the ground to hover about two metres in the air, in front of all the Heroes. I sneak glances into the crowd, between cowls and capes, but I can't see the OK Team anywhere.

'Hi, Heroes. Thanks for coming.' the Southern Cross floats effortlessly, hands on hips. 'As far as we can tell, almost every registered Hero in the state is here, apart from two Level Gs called "The Slacker Twins", who said they might show up later. Naturally, this entire meeting is subject to the top level of Hero Security. At this stage, the only non-Heroes aware of the threat are military personnel and a couple of psychics who got lucky.'

'But what is the threat?' asks a female Hero in the front row. She has a crimson cape, matching mask and gloves, and blonde hair piled high on her head. I have no idea who she is but I like her sense of fashion.

'I won't beat about the bush,' the Southern Cross says. 'Melbourne faces a potentially terminal threat from a massive asteroid.'

'An asteroid!' exclaims a Hero a few chairs down from me.

'Fly fast does the stone yet large is the void,' answers his companion. I realise it's the Crypto Twins.

'If you'll all look to the ceiling, I can show you,' the Southern Cross says.

We all look up – I hear a female voice yell, 'Quack!' – and we're gazing at a virtual screen hanging in the air, showing an enormous lump of rock twirling in space.

'This asteroid is huge,' continues the Southern Cross. 'If it impacts, it will take out the city centre and more than five kilometres of suburbs in any direction. While Melbourne would be obliterated instantly, the rest of the world would probably be doomed from the fallout.'

'But it won't happen, right?' says a small beetle a few rows in front of me.

'No, BugMan. It won't because Golden Boy is going to take it out, on our behalf.'

There is a burst of applause as Golden Boy flies into the air to float next to the Southern Cross. I can't help but think he looks pale as he waves to acknowledge the applause – as pale as you can look with golden light shining all around you.

A Hero asks, 'How do you plan to do it, Golden Boy?'

'I have, um, a number of strategies that I'm considering at this time,' Golden Boy says. 'Point of impact is twenty hours away, so we have some breathing space.'

Mr Fabulous stands up, dead centre of the Hero crowd and three rows from the front. I hear the murmur as everyday heroes spot the Hall of Fame legend.

'Golden Boy, this is a big moment for you. You must be excited,' the old man says, staring hard at the Triple A.

Golden Boy hovers, looking blankly at Mr Fabulous, then swallows hard and says, 'Um, excuse me.'

Just like that, he isn't there any more. That's super speed for you.

Everybody looks at one another in surprise. In the silence I hear Ace say to the Southern Cross, 'That was an unexpected shuffle of the deck. I hope Golden Boy isn't a wild card to send up against a meteor.'

And then, not quite as quickly (so we can all see the blur as he tries to super-speed out of there), Mr Fabulous is gone as well.

There is a low murmur of voices, including the odd honk, musical sting or explosion, as Heroes talk among themselves about what just happened. I stand to stretch my legs, and it's then I notice the OK Team sitting towards the back of the crowd on the other side of the room.

Man, I'm thinking, Mr Fabulous is so full of himself that he doesn't even let the team sit with him when real Heroes are around.

Just as I'm gazing at them, Liarbird happens to look my way. Our eyes meet and I find it hard to breathe. It might be some evil plot by a super-villain to suck the air from the room, but, then again, I often have trouble breathing when I look at Liarbird. I see her perfect lips move and I almost smile as I imagine her saying, 'I can't see Focus.' Sure enough Torch, Cannonball and Yesterday start looking around the room. Cannonball says loudly, 'I'll be able to see him from the sky,' poses, and then shoots clear to the other side of the huge space, smacking into a far wall. So nothing has changed there.

I can feel my visibility has gone, which is a shame because I'd quite like Torch to see me and to think how well and happy I look. I don't know if I can pull off 'well' or 'happy' as a look, but I'm willing to try. Liarbird is still looking in my direction and I'm tempted to go over and say hello but then I remember that I'm supposed to be mad with them all, and resentful because they're still in the team and I'm not.

As I turn back to face the Southern Cross at the front of the room, I hear Yesterday's high young voice clearly, over the rising sound of the crowd still discussing Golden Boy's exit. 'I knew Focus would be here.'

There is a golden flash and guess what, Golden Boy is back, standing right next to the Southern Cross, about two metres above our heads and with his arms folded casually. Mr Fabulous also creakily super-speeds into the room and takes his seat down the front.

'Sorry about that,' Golden Boy says. 'I thought I heard a cry for help . . . it turns out it was, um, just the meteor begging for mercy. That it won't get!'

A few Heroes cheer and there are a few laughs. The Southern Cross wraps things up by telling us to stay alert, leave the actual world-saving to Golden Boy, but look to handle his giant share of the everyday crime-fighting between us so he can concentrate on what he has to do.

Heroes start to stand or fly or spin, and I suddenly realise that I'm not ready to talk to the OK Team members. The thought of facing them makes me invisible so fast that I walk straight through the crowd like a ghost and through the wall of the room. If I can stay out of whack long enough, I might be able to walk straight through the power plant's outer wall. I think about what might happen if I met the Team.

'Life's a lot better without you,' Torch might say. Completely invisible, I walk through another wall.

'Torch is a great leader!' Yesterday could add. Still nothing but a transparent cloud.

'Much better than you,' says Switchy. I walk clean through more brick.

And then I see Golden Boy and the Southern Cross standing in a patch of light shining through a grimy window. Even Golden Boy's usual glow is dimmed and he's strangely slumped. They have their heads together, talking quietly. I check that I am still completely out of focus, then drift a little closer, like the mist I am.

Golden Boy is speaking. 'You're the only one I can say this to, Cross. What if I can't do it?'

'You have to. Nobody else can.'

'But who says I can?'

'You're Triple A. You have powers others only dream of. Why can't you do it?'

'This meteor is huge. I'm so small. I've never tackled anything that big.'

'There has to be a first time.'

'I know everybody is talking behind my back about my lack of world-saves. It's like this blip on my record and I haven't joined the truly elite Heroes because of it.'

'Who's talking? And who cares. Take out the meteor and silence them.'

'But they might be right. Maybe I don't belong in that elite group of Heroes. Astonishinglygreatgirl would just blast straight through it without blinking. I don't know if I'm capable.'

The Southern Cross frowns and thinks for a moment. 'What did Mr Fabulous have to say when you both took off?'

Golden Boy smiles grimly. 'He told me that I was being weak and to get my act together. Said if he was my age, he would have not only beaten the meteor but eaten it for breakfast. Said it was *only* the size of a small mountain, so why worry?'

'Hmmm, so "super supportive" isn't one of his powers then,' the Southern Cross says, shaking his head.

'Apparently not. He was rough. Told me I was a disgrace to the Triple As and threatened to have a word with Gotham about my status.'

At which point I get angry enough to snap back into some kind of visibility, with the slightly pleasing result, when I think about it later, that I shock both big-time Heroes with my appearance.

'What? Where did you come from?' says Golden Boy.

'Have you been listening to us? How much did you hear?'

'Practically nothing,' I lie. 'I was just leaving the meeting, passing through walls, you know.' I shrug like I actually know how to do this. 'But I did hear what you just said about Mr Fabulous. I wanted to say that the old guy is the worst mentor in the world. He's so full of himself and how great he used to be years ago that he has no patience for anybody. He kicked me out of my own team!'

Golden Boy snaps a golden finger. 'That's where I know you from, kid. You were part of that pathetic new mob, the All Right Gang.'

'The OK Team, actually, but yeah, I was. Until he said I was crap. But I'm not crap, and even if I am, I'm working to get better. I am a Hero, and some crusty old fossil from Gotham isn't going to tell me otherwise.'

They both stare at me, trying to take in this outburst. I realise I'd better bring things back to the point. 'Golden Boy, it doesn't matter what he says. You have to believe in yourself. You've been my favourite Hero forever. You can do anything. That meteor is toast.'

My brain catches up to inform me that I've just been dweebish enough to tell Golden Boy face-to-golden-face that he's my favourite Hero, and of course my body goes wildly out of whack in embarrassment. Which is incredibly lucky because it gives me my escape, through the last three walls to the street.

'A Hero is a Hero,' I say. 'No matter what.' And then I'm gone.

To them, it probably looks like I deliberately turned invisible. Which is cool.

It's been a big night. The strangest thing is that as I pass through the final, massive outer wall and head down Spencer Street towards Collins Street and a tram stop, I could swear I hear an old man chuckling.

SUPER NEWSREADER: Only sixteen hours now until anticipated asteroid impact in Melbourne, Australia. Local military forces and politicians are trying to decide when to inform the general population of the threat, while Gotham pleads for silence. There's been no word from local Triple A-er Golden Boy, and nervous Gotham Hero executives are wondering whether to send in some global Triple A heavyweights to make sure this asteroid doesn't get to land. More on that story as it comes to hand.

CHAPTER 27
THE COMEBACK KID

The next day at school I overhear some classmates talking about Scumm not turning up. None of his henchmen have either. Seven kids wagging at once is something even the teachers can't ignore, and apparently all sorts of phone calls have been flying around between the principal and parents.

Me? I keep looking at the sky, wondering what's going on up there. By the end of the school day, we could all be dead if Golden Boy or another Hero doesn't take that mountainous rock apart. If it does end up being another Hero, Golden Boy is finished. He'll be a laughing stock. Who knows, that could even make him a little less superior when it comes to judging start-up Heroes like me.

At recess, I'm sitting under a tree, enjoying the sunshine, wondering if my parents found it strange that I gave them both an extra big hug as I left for school. I even told them I loved them, which should have been a sure sign something was going on. I thought about not spending potentially my last day on Earth at school, but couldn't think of anything better to do. Hero TV was becoming depressing, with increasingly urgent news flashes about the meteor.

I have my eyes closed when I sense something large blocking my sunshine. Scumm? No, he's not here. I blink my eyes open and there's Frederick Fodder, standing with Simon Fondue, looking down at me.

'Mind if we sit with you, Hazy?' says Simon.

'Sure,' I say. Now Frederick's little sister, Alexandra, is walking over here and – my heart starts beating – she's with a tall, willowy girl with ghost-white hair in a ponytail. Ali Fraudulent.

I start to blur. I might fall through the tree. What's going on?

The four of them sit around me so we're in a circle. As always, Simon is kind of peeping at me from under his long hair but he seems to be smiling.

'Hazy, we miss you,' he says. 'We want you back in the team.'

'Huh?' I say. 'What team?'

'Please don't be like that,' Alexandra pleads. 'Don't act as if the team never existed. Strong is the Hero who turns the other cheek. Fab was wrong to throw you out, and we all want you back in.'

'Even I don't like fighting bad guys without my old companion alongside me,' says Frederick. At that moment it finally hits me. I'm looking at Cannonball in his everyday alter-ego. Frederick is Cannonball! They are one and the same.

I feel like the biggest idiot in the world. There they are – right in front of me, and they've been there all along, every day, and I hadn't seen them. Little Yesterday, shy Torch, stocky Cannonball and . . . I fall completely out of focus as I make the connection between Ali, the girl who never speaks . . . because she knows if she did she would tell nothing but lies . . . and Liarbird.

'How is your hair white as Ali, but dark as Liarbird?' I ask stupidly.

'I don't wear a wig, genius,' she says, smiling.

That sends me further out of whack. I'm a cloud.

Luckily Yesterday has misread my fast-vanishing appearance. 'See,' she tells Ali, putting her fingers to her temples. 'I told you he wouldn't go for this idea.'

'No, Alexandra, you're wrong,' I say, and I'm clear again.

In fact, I know instinctively that I'm crystal clear. And I even know why.

They gasp as I hold up my left hand. It's not there, but the rest of me is. Now I hold up my right hand and click my fingers as it vanishes and my left hand reappears. I click those fingers and the left hand goes, right hand appears again. My teammates are slack jawed in admiration.

'You're wrong, because I want nothing more in the world than to be part of the team again,' I say. 'The only question is whether you want me. Mr Fabulous made it pretty clear that he didn't. Where do you stand?'

Frederick Fodder, aka Cannonball, looks over a shoulder to check no kids are around and leans in so he can speak quietly. 'We don't just want you back, Focus. We want you back as leader more than a polar bear wants fish for dinner.'

'Are you serious?' I ask. 'What about Torch?'

Simon pushes some hair out of his eyes and looks me straight in the eye. 'The truth is, I never wanted to be leader, Hazy. Mr Fabulous wanted me to be, because of who I am, my family, my Hero bloodlines. I'm having enough trouble being anything more than a novelty human candle without trying to lead the team.'

I'm trembling now, but I turn to Ali Fraudulent, gazing quietly at me with those deep grey eyes of hers. 'What about you, Ali? Do you want me back?'

She doesn't immediately reply. Instead her face sort of flickers and she frowns and she's still looking at me but there is this sense of a huge internal battle going on.

At last, she says, 'Yes, Focus, I want you back.'

I'm crushed. I can't look anybody in the eye and my visibility is going again.

'Well, sorry guys, but unless the whole team wants me back, forget it.'

'Hazy,' Yesterday's hand is on my fading arm. 'Liarbird meant it.'

I look at her and at Ali, whose eyes are pleading with me to understand.

'She actually *does* want you back,' says Alexandra.

Ali nods. 'I do,' she whispers.

I gape. 'You're telling the truth?'

She nods again. Too many words is obviously too much effort.

'That's fantastic,' I say. 'How long have you been able to do this?'

'Decades,' she says, and then realises what she has said, grins and shrugs at me.

'Actually, that wasn't just the first time ever.' She looks apologetic again.

I'm grinning. 'It's fine, Liarbird. Relax and tell lies for a while. It will be easier. I can't believe you did it!'

'I sensed she was about to,' says Alexandra.

'You did not,' says her brother, rolling his eyes.

'I did so. Like, right before she told the truth, I thought: she's going to tell the truth.'

'Prove it.'

'I don't have to prove it. Prove you can fly straight, Nerderick.'

'Guys,' I say. 'There's just one, actually two things. What about Mr Fabulous?'

'We sacked him,' says Cannonball casually.

'You what???'

'We sacked him like a restaurant gets rid of runny soup.'

'I wouldn't say we sacked him,' Torch says, giving Frederick a look. 'He was pretty cool about it, actually. Didn't even seem surprised. We thanked him for his help but said we'd rather find our own way. After he got rid of you, we all felt uncomfortable.'

'I saw him sitting away from you at the meeting but thought he must have told you to sit down the back.'

'No, we chose not to sit with him,' says Alexandra/Yesterday. I'm still having trouble getting used to seeing these schoolkids as my teammates.

'What about Switchy? Where does he stand? I'm not coming back unless it's unanimous that you guys want me.'

Suddenly the tree behind me starts to shake. I turn in surprise and notice the trunk has changed to a slightly red shade of brown. There's a pop and the tree becomes a rubbish bin, then another pop and we're all looking at a small black dog.

'I want you back 3.5 million per cent, Focus,' says the dog. 'We're a team and teammates should stick together absolutely for all time.'

I look at them all. They're staring back at me. I say to Liarbird, 'You really want me back?' and that internal fight takes place and she manages to nod. We grin at each other.

I put my hand out and it's sharply in focus.

'I'm OK,' I say.

Simon, Alexandra, Ali, Frederick and the small black dog put their hands, and paw, on top of mine.

'You're OK!' they say.

'We're OK,' we finish. And I realise that Liarbird didn't mumble her usual disagreement.

The OK Team rides again. I'm so happy my heart is soaring above the clouds somewhere, just like a meteor.

'We should get out of school,' I say. 'That meteor must be getting close. I want to know what's going on.'

CHAPTER 28

THE OK TEAM RIDES AGAIN

L iarbird gets us out of there. We're worried the teachers will be able to trace back the number if she uses her mobile phone, so she sneaks out the front gate, runs down the street to a pay phone and then phones the principal's office. She says she's my mother and I have to leave for a dentist's appointment. Then she rings back, and in a different voice says that Frederick Fodder is required for an acrobatic school audition, at short notice. And so on, until we're all free and clear. We change into our costumes and I try to see Ali Fraudulent, with her ghost-white hair, in dark-haired, purple-suited Liarbird. When I think about it, they both look good. Or she does, either way, more to the point.

Walking down the street, I think about how long we've all been at school together without me realising who they actually were. And about how many clues have been right in front of me. What a loser.

'Hey Torch,' I say, when Simon and I are a little away from the rest of the group. 'How long did it take you to realise I was Focus?'

Simon looks at me from under his hair and smiles. 'Don't take this the wrong way, but there aren't that many kids in the area born out of focus.'

'Oh right, I guess. It, um, took me a while to work out who you guys were,'

'Frederick and I fessed up to one another pretty quickly,' Torch says. 'I put two and two together when I saw Frederick fly for a mark in footy and land metres away. I pulled him aside and lit my finger and he almost fell over. It was pretty funny.'

'What about Ali? I mean, Liarbird?'

'That was Yesterday. She told Frederick that she had worked out why Ali never talks. She reckons it was her ability "to see" that worked it out, but we reckon it's just some girl vibe and she got lucky.'

We head back to Torch's house. We're a bit nervous about running into Mr Fabulous, but Torch says he's not the sort to hold a grudge. It turns out he's not even there, but lots of other Heroes are: mostly Papa Torch's crusty old mates, but also a few other heroes of different ages, powers and gradings.

Everybody is gathered in the living room around Channel 78737. As we find some space where you can see the screen, I notice the bookshelf next to me shift slightly. I squint and see that it's actually Leon standing in front of it, melded into the background as ever.

'How are you?' he says.

'Brilliant! Never been better!' I say honestly.

'I see you're back with your team. That's great.'

'You knew I wasn't?'

'Focus,' he says, with an edge to it. 'We know everything, remember?'

'Do you know if Golden Boy is going to take out this meteor before we're all dust?'

'No,' he admits. 'I don't know that. Golden Boy is missing. I'll feel bad for him, but I think they're going to have to send in some overseas Triple As. Get the job done. This is getting too tight.'

'When do they let the non-Hero world know about the threat?'

Leon laughs. 'They probably won't. This kind of thing – well, not this dramatic, but potentially Earth-threatening – happens about ten times a year and non-Heroes haven't got a clue.'

'What if the meteor lands?'

Leon shrugs. 'It's still better, isn't it? They'll never know what hit them.'

Channel 78737's news flash music starts up, so we turn to the TV. Papa Torch tells everybody to shut up and stop that chattering. Then realises it's Ice Man's frozen teeth that are chattering, as usual, and apologises.

On the screen, a male Hero newsreader in a full deep blue cowl and cape appears.

215

NEWSREADER: Less than two hours now until the asteroid impact zone. Still no word from our teams covering Golden Boy's home and other haunts. Gotham has an emergency meeting scheduled for one hour from now.

Meanwhile, a Hero haze has been placed around the entire city.

A picture of an old man in a trenchcoat and sunglasses, smoke steaming from his nostrils, appears on the screen. He looks vaguely familiar.

NEWSREADER: Another major hero story is emerging, believe it or not, in the shadow of the asteroid. Hero Hall of Famer Mr Fabulous has been kidnapped.

Yes, that's right. The old timer, currently in Melbourne to assist Golden Boy during his first world save, has been nabbed by an old nemesis, Scorch, who hadn't been seen for three decades before briefly being spotted yesterday. Scorch is being assisted by some rising young Villains, led by somebody calling himself 'Moonface'. We believe Mr Fabulous is being held hostage at what used to be the Planetarium at the old Melbourne Science Museum.

Local Hero Southern Cross had this to say . . .

SOUTHERN CROSS: Scorch and these young punks have terrible timing.

We're worried for Mr Fabulous, but we've decided to give him the respect he deserves. We assume that a legend of his standing won't let anything too bad happen down in the museum until we have seen off this meteor and can turn our full attention to his rescue.

NEWSREADER: So there you have it. Hang tight, Fab, and if there's anything or anybody left in Melbourne a couple of hours from now, we'll see if we can get around to a rescue.

It's all happening down under.

The image on the screen changes to the huge old science museum, topped by a rusty satellite dish. Several Villains can be seen for a moment, tiny against the massive dish, waving and yelling at the flying camera.

NEWSREADER: Hero TV will have a remote camera at the scene between now and the asteroid, just in case. Good luck, Mr Fabulous.

The newsflash ends, and I realise I'm standing.

'Captain Rewind, were you recording that?' I ask.

'Of course,' says a Hero with white hair and a giant TV screen where his chest should be. 'Why, son?'

'Can you please rewind to that shot of the science museum? Where you could see the satellite dish?'

The screen on his chest comes to life, showing what we just saw, but now scrolling back a few seconds. I can't believe I'm working with such a local Hero legend. I take the moment to say to him, 'I'm Focus, by the way. A friend of Papa Torch's grandson. It's nice to meet you. I've always been a fan.'

'Thanks, kid. Now what did you want to see?'

'Can you zoom in on the dish itself? Where the bad guys are . . . That's it. Closer . . .'

'Focus? What's going on?' It's Torch, with the rest of the OK Team behind him. We're all looking at Captain Rewind's screen.

'There!' I say, pointing, and my thumb is a little blurry in excitement and fear. 'Look, in front of the other villains. Recognise that guy?'

He's jumping up and down, making rude gestures. We can't see his face because he's wearing a huge white mask that is shaped like the Moon, and a black bodysuit with a half moon on the front, but we all know the body language and the massive musclebound body. We know who we're looking at.

'Scooby Doo!' says Liarbird.

'Scumm,' says Torch. 'We should have known.'

'Yeah,' I say. 'He and all his lughead mates not being at school today, of all days. It's up to us, team.'

'What?' says Yesterday, looking shocked but a bit excited too.

'We're going to save Mr Fabulous.'

'Are you nuts, Focus?' says Torch. 'We're not ready. That's a job for real Heroes.'

'We are real Heroes. The moment we choose to be. That's what I've finally realised. That's why I can finally do what Mr Fabulous asked and make different parts of myself disappear when I want them to. It's all about believing in yourself. I AM a Hero and I CAN control my power.'

They stare at me. Then Cannonball suddenly grabs me a in a bear hug. 'Yeah! A Hero is a Hero. No matter what!!!'

'Nice speech, kid,' says Papa Torch. 'You finally get it.'

He creaks out of his chair and shuffles over to his grandson. 'You want to know a secret, Simon?' he says gently. 'When I started, all those endless years ago . . . guess what my only power was? My first sign that I was a Hero?'

'No way!' says Torch. 'Are you serious?'

'Yes,' says the old man, flicking a wrinkled finger until a flame appears. 'Only this.'

Torch looks as if this is the line he's waited his whole life to hear. He calmly nods, points his much younger index finger, and shoots a burst of flame across the room as though it's the most natural thing in the world. A candle bursts neatly to life on the dining room table, exactly where he'd aimed.

I high-five him – and the rest of the team – and we charge out of the room. A gaggle of ageing, past-it Heroes cheer like a footy crowd from Papa Torch's front patio as the OK Team runs across the lawn.

'Leon, you want to come with us?' I ask.

'No, I'm going to find out what's happening with Golden Boy. Call me if you need me.'

I nod, and check the OK Team is still all there.

It's time to go to work.

SCORCH

AGE: 81 years old
VILLAIN GRADING: Category 7
KNOWN POWERS:
➤ Ability to shoot molten lava and flames from nostrils
KNOWN CATCHCRIES:
'A good Hero is a melted Hero'

CHAPTER 29
MOMENT OF TRUTH

The science museum is across town, on the other side of the West Gate Bridge. With an hour and a half before the meteor is due to hit, we don't have time to catch public transport.

'Switchy,' I say. 'Make like a helicopter.'

'Focus . . .' he says.

'Don't think. Don't question. Just do.' I stare him down. 'Switchy, you can be whoever or whatever you want to be . . . including yourself. Be 500 per cent sure that you're capable of it, for me. Right now, we need a helicopter.'

He takes a deep breath, nods once, turns red, shakes, and suddenly I'm staring at a wheelbarrow.

'Come on, Switchy. You can do it!'

The wheelbarrow shakes, turns red, and POP!, I'm staring at a helicopter.

'Rock and roll!' I say. 'Everybody, in. Let's go, Switchy.'

Switchy's made himself into a fast helicopter and we're there inside of five minutes, touching down outside the museum. The enormous bluestone building is at least five storeys high and half a city block in size. I take a few moments to look at the building, to look at our surroundings, to think of a plan.

My team gathers around me, waiting for instructions. I can't help but enjoy how 'right' this feels, and how natural leadership suddenly is.

'Before we start, everybody, hands and gloves in,' I say, extending my right hand in front of me. 'You know what to do. I'm OK!'

'You're OK!'

'WE'RE OK!!!!!!'

We say it like we mean it. I get shivers, and not from my power.

I make my hand vanish then reappear, and they all look surprised, then smile.

'See,' I say. 'Nothing to it.'

I turn to those grey eyes.

'Liarbird. In a moment you're going to lie your way in there, with Switchy. I'll already be in there, and so will Cannonball. There's one thing we all have to be really clear on. Liarbird, it's fantastic that you're starting to control when you tell the truth and when you lie, but telling the truth doesn't come naturally for you yet. Under pressure, during a battle, I think it will be easier and more natural for you to lie. If any of us ask you a question, we're going to assume any answers you give us are your usual lies. OK?'

She frowns, thinks, and finally says, 'Yes, got it.'

'No,' I say, a little sharply. 'What did I just say? Tell me again, have you got it?'

This time she nods, and doesn't hesitate. 'No, I have no idea what you're talking about.'

'Good,' I grin. 'Right, Cannonball. There's a broken window four floors up. It looks narrow, but it's probably big enough for you to get through if you don't touch the broken glass. I want you in there, noiselessly, and ready to act when I call you. OK?'

Cannonball looks way up the wall to the tiny broken window. 'You want me to fly straight up there and through that window?'

'Yep. And you will, because you can. Believe in yourself, Cannonball. I believe in you.'

He nods and poses a very Heroic, typical Cannonball pose. 'Right, then. LET'S FIRE THE CANNON!'

'Mr Fabulous said you weren't allowed to say that,' says his sister, hands on hips.

'He's not here though, is he,' says Cannonball. 'And anyway, as of now, I'm being who I want to be. Just like an elk.'

And with that he takes off, soaring straight as an arrow for the window, and through. Without a sound.

'Wow, he's in,' I say, trying to keep the surprise out of my voice.

Torch claps a hand on my back. 'This self-belief stuff actually works, Focus.'

'Who would have thought?' I grin and point to six thick cables hung between the nearest power pole and the museum. 'Torch, can you use your flame to cut those powerlines?'

'Definitely,' he says. We compare our watches and agree on an exact time, then he runs over there.

'OK, Switchy. Turn yourself into whatever Liarbird needs you to be, and go with Liarbird to the front door. Liarbird, do what you do best. I'll see you in there.'

I'm about to head for the building itself when Yesterday's voice stops me.

'Focus? What about me?'

I turn and she looks very small, very young.

'Right now, Yesterday, I can't think of a role for you,' I reply honestly.

She sadly puts her fingers to her temples. 'I can tell that you sense my power is crap and I'm a total fraud.'

'No, Yesterday, that's not true.'

'It is true, and maybe you're right. Look at Cannonball, and Torch, and you! You can all use actual superpowers.'

'Yesterday,' I say. 'I've got to go now, but hear this: If you say you can see into the past, or the future, or the next room, then I'm going to believe you. Just because there isn't a role for you right now, in this particular operation, doesn't mean your time won't come.'

She nods, looking at the ground. 'I've heard that. Cometh the moment, cometh the man, or woman.'

'That's right. In fact, don't stay here. Go with Liarbird and Switchy, and once inside, focus as hard as you can on the vibes of the battle. Let me know if you sense anything is about to happen before it happens.'

'Look into the future, Focus?'

'You bet, and if you do it, we'll have to change your super name. But concentrate hard, Yesterday, and believe. You could save a life.'

'Sweet,' she says, smiling now.

'We need to go. Come on!'

CHAPTER 30
TO THE RESCUE

*T*he wall is thick – at least a metre of brick stands between me on the outside and whatever is inside. Calmly, I lose focus and walk straight through it. Still invisible, I let my eyes adjust to the sudden lack of light and assess my surroundings. I'm in a small room with the door open. I can hear voices further inside.

I move into the corridor and head in the same direction the others took on the outside. At a corner, I hear voices quite close. It's Liarbird.

'Well, all I can say is that you are the least excited contest winners I have ever encountered. Most people would be ecstatic to have won a lifetime supply of doughnuts and would be saying to me, please, oh please, wheel that big trolley of doughnuts in here this minute so we can dive in and eat until we're sick!'

'It's not a good time right now,' says a husky teenage voice.

'Yeah, come back later, toots.'

'I love it when people call me toots,' says Liarbird pleasantly. 'Well, I'm taking the trolley away, but I'm not coming back later. As you'll remember from when you bought your ticket, if you refuse the prize then it goes to the runner-up.'

'I don't even remember buying the ticket,' mumbles one of the male voices.

'Maybe it was Scu – I mean, Moonface?'

'He'll be mad if we turn this away.'

'He loves doughnuts.'

'You've had your chance. See ya,' says Liarbird, her voice sounding further away.

'Hey! Wait a minute!'

'Yeah. Come back with them doughnuts.'

'It's "those" doughnuts,' Liarbird says, her voice getting closer again. 'Honestly, where do you boys go to school?'

'Just shut up and put the trolley over there,' says one of the boys.

'OK, and while I'm at it, do you want to see a trick?'

'Listen, you dumb chick, just get lost, will you?'

'I like being called a "dumb chick" even more than "toots",' Liarbird says happily.

'Whatever. Don't let the door hit your butt on the way out.'

Liarbird giggles in a very un-Liarbirdish way. 'You're funny! Here's my trick . . . See the trolley? It bites.'

'How can a trolley bite?'

'Yeah, that's stupi –'

Clang! Kwong!

I turn the corner and see two boys unconscious on the ground. Switchy is a trolley carrying boxes of doughnuts, but with the handle now transformed into two massive metal flowers with giant teeth. The flowers are swaying from where they bonked Scumm's henchmen on the head.

'A lethal, metal-flower-headed doughnut trolley,' I say. 'Creative.'

'Thought I'd have some fun,' says Switchy, changing into a black-uniformed ninja. 'It was 162 per cent successful.'

'Well, look at you mastering your talent!' I say, grinning. 'And Liarbird, you were fantastic.'

Liarbird gives me a smile and opens the door again so Yesterday can slip through. The four of us walk deeper and deeper into the old museum.

'I sense we're getting close,' says Yesterday.

I motion to the others to stop, then creep forward around a corner, and there is the villainous gang, with Mr Fabulous in the middle. I duck back to where the others are. 'We're there. Yesterday, was that a guess, or did you know?'

'I'm honestly not sure,' she says, wide-eyed.

Switchy changes into a periscope leading to a TV screen, and sticks his head around the corner so Liarbird and Yesterday can have a look at the enemy too. I make my head invisible – the party trick works! – and take another look for myself.

It's not good.

Mr Fabulous is tied to a chair with chains that are at least a metre thick and cover his whole body. You can only just see the top of his head and the toes of his old boots. The chains are glowing green, as though powered by some unearthly energy.

'Do you think it's Fabu-nite, the one substance said to weaken Mr Fabulous?' Switchy's voice whispers from somewhere below the periscope's lens.

'No idea,' I say, honestly. 'Isn't Fabu-nite blue? I wish Torch was with us. He'd know. Which reminds me – he's due to cut the power in one minute.'

'Focus,' Yesterday says, 'how do we get rid of the weapons?'

It's a good point. Not only is Mr Fabulous wrapped in giant green-glowing chains, he is also targeted by more army weapons than your average soldier would expect to see in three lifetimes. Two of Moonface's henchmen are pointing what look like handguns at the old Hero. Another two are pointing bazookas, which are like rocket-launchers that balance on a person's shoulder. Next to them is a teenager holding a sub-machine gun, pointing at Mr Fabulous's chest.

Scumm himself, still wearing his enormous moon-themed helmet, has a remote control that appears to be connected to the four cannons that are also pointing at Mr Fabulous.

Beyond Moonface, there is a full-sized tank, its turret pointing directly at our old mentor.

Beyond that is a fighter jet, with all missiles pointed straight at his chest.

Behind all this, the arch Villain Scorch, aka William Weld, is wandering around in the background, muttering and occasionally blasting a chair with what looks like extreme heat from his nose, both nostrils, melting whatever it touches.

We might be out of our depth. I feel myself start to blur but refuse to let it happen. My body becomes more or less sharp again, through sheer will.

'A plan,' I say. 'Hmmm. Switchy, you need to be a bird.'

I turn to face the others and Yesterday has a small brown swallow sitting on her forearm. Its head cocks, listening.

'Nice,' I say. 'OK, fly to the broken window and tell Cannonball he has to take out Weld, I mean Scorch. He's a veteran, highly-graded Villain so Cannonball is not to underestimate him. He has to fly fast and keep moving around, so Scorch can't get a clean shot at him with his nose-rays. Got it? Meanwhile, we'll rescue Mr Fabulous.'

'How?' asks Liarbird. 'There are only 437 of us.'

'I'm working on that,' I say. 'Go, Switchy.'

The swallow chirrups quietly and suddenly flaps its wings, flying in a lurching path towards the roof.

'What's that?' I hear one of Scumm's henchmen yell.

'Just a bird,' says Scumm's voice. 'Relax. This old place must be full of nests and stuff.'

'How long until they pay the ransom?' asks another henchman.

'Soon,' says an old voice. It must be Scorch. 'I don't know why Heroes aren't crawling all over this place. Surely Golden Boy or somebody has taken out the meteor by now. We need to get their attention.'

'We could fire a rocket through the roof,' says Scumm.

'And give them an easy entry point, right on top of us. Genius,' says Scorch.

'I was just making a suggestion.' Moonface sounds sulky.

I peer around the corner. All the guns, rockets, cannons, tanks and jet are still pointing right at Mr Fabulous.

And that's when Torch does his thing outside and the lights cut out.

'Hey!' yells a henchman. 'What's going on?'

Scorch, from the far side of the room, is in control. 'Keep your guns on Mr Fabulous. Just aim for the glowing chains. Moonface, can you see anything?'

Moonface's massive helmet is glowing, giving him his own light source. I have to admit I'm impressed. There's no way a blockhead like Scumm has come up with this on his own.

'A fuse must have blown or something. I'll start the emergency generator you brought along, boss.'

It's time for me to move. Still invisible, I leave my hiding spot and follow Moonface's glowing orb. He crouches and flicks a switch and there's the hum of a power generator. As the lights come back on, Moonface straightens up and I let him see my head, floating all alone in space above my invisible body.

'What??? Fuzzy-Wuzzy Freak Show??' he yells in surprise.

'Nope, Scumm-bucket. The name's Focus,' I say, and I swing a punch at him. My arm turns out to be completely blurred through the usual fear and it swings harmlessly past.

Moonface starts to laugh, and I feel the doubt creeping in.

No!

'A Hero is a Hero,' I say to myself, somewhere deep in my fuzzy head. 'No matter what!'

And then my right arm is perfectly solid for the time it takes to belt the top of Scumm's helmet so that it covers his eyes. As he blunders around, losing his balance, my suddenly-solid left hand grabs him by the back of his costume, feels around and gives him the wedgie to end all wedgies.

'Ouuuuuwwwwwwww,' says Scumm. I boot him in the backside and he collides heavily with the massive framework of a tank and lies quietly.

Scorch has seen me. 'One of your little hobbies, hey, Fabulous. Well, he's toast now.'

I see Scorch lift his head so his nostrils are pointing towards me. A ray of pure energy and heat passes through where I would be if I wasn't now invisible. I feel it warming my scattered molecules as it passes.

233

'Man, you must have a nasty time if you get a head cold,' I say from within my unharmed cloud.

'Dodge this, you freak!' Scorch screams and fires again. Still a mist, I watch the blast melt a chair behind me.

'How come your name is "Scorch" and not "Sinus"?' I ask. 'Or "Hot Snot"?'

'Why, you little . . .'

I'm feeling so good about things that I accidentally become vaguely solid and Scorch sees his chance, nostrils aimed to line me up.

'Hey,' yells Liarbird. She, Yesterday and Torch, who has found his way into the building, can now be seen against the far wall. 'Scorch, don't look down!'

Scorch does at the exact moment he fires, and burns his foot with his heat blast.

'Ow!' he says, hoping around. 'Oww, owww, owwww. I hate it when I do that.'

The henchmen have all been watching this like a football match, fingers itching the triggers of their guns, but unsure which way to fire or what to do. Now, with Liarbird, Torch and Yesterday in the open, they see their chance, and I'm horrified as several of the guns swing away from the glowing chains and towards my friends.

Until one of the tanks – wasn't there only one tank? – the second tank turns red and shakes and pops, suddenly changing into a massive bed mattress covering the sky above all the henchmen, the remaining tank and the jet. As the henchmen swing their guns towards the floating mattress, it turns red, shakes and, POP!, becomes a thick sludge, washing the bad guys and all their weaponry off their feet. It sets hard, trapping them helplessly. Up one end is a multi-coloured mask and a big smile.

'Nice work, Switchy,' I grin.

'Now you're really for it,' says Scorch, and he somehow flips his head way, way back – further than a normal neck should enable a head to tilt – as his nose seems to grow until his nostrils are like two car exhaust pipes sticking out of his face.

We watch, astonished, as his entire body begins to glow red and shake as he prepares to fire at Switchy's hardened form.

MOONFACE

AGE: 14 years old
VILLIAN GRADING: Category 1, Level B
KNOWN POWERS: ➤ Sub-super strength ➤ Willingness to hurt
KNOWN CATCHCRIES:
'What are you looking at, freak?'

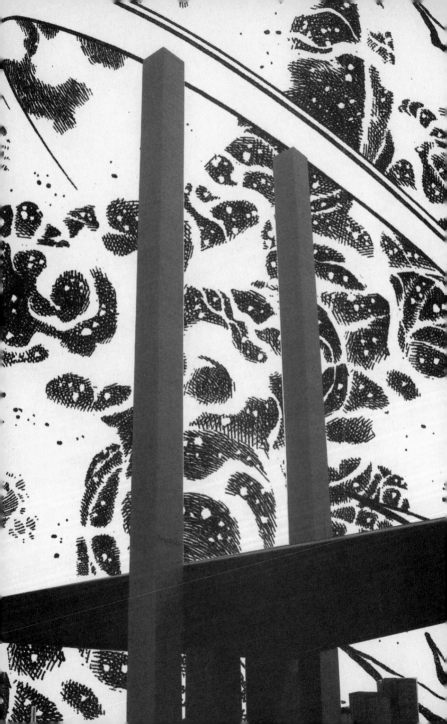

CHAPTER 31
BETTER THAN OK

Way up in the rafters, a young but bold voice hollers, 'LET'S FIRE THE CANNON!'

My original Hero partner flies like the little cannonball that he is, red circle shining on his chest and black helmet heading straight for Scorch who is tilting his head upside down to get a clear shot at him. The super-villain lets fly with an almighty energy burst, but Cannonball neatly changes his flight path ever so slightly to watch the heat blur past. Scorch fires again, and then lets fly with a constant stream of lightning, but Cannonball is swooping and rising and falling so the bad guy can never quite line him up.

And then Cannonball dips, grabs a bucket of water he just spotted, and dumps it over Scorch's head. Water pours into the Villain's upside-down nostrils and he sneezes violently, sending flaming snot and steam flying in all directions. Scorch flips his head back to where it should be, and what looks like volcanic lava pours out of his nose. He's squealing and crying.

Cannonball plants the bucket on Scorch's head and bonks it with a fist. The vanquished Villain slumps to the ground.

'Well, that wasn't gross,' says Liarbird.

'I know it's not my place to say and everything,' says Torch, 'but you took your time to tackle Scorch, Cannonball.'

Cannonball looks almost sheepish, especially for him. 'I was worried that if I yelled "Let's fire the cannon", they would think I meant the ones down here.'

'Hey, people, guess what? We won!' It's Switchy, changing from giant Silly Putty to a tall, clear-skinned youth of about seventeen. All around him, groaning henchmen are sprawled.

'We've still got to rescue Mr Fabulous!' I say. 'Torch, the chains.'

Torch points both hands at the huge pile of glowing chains and lets fly with a blast of fire that burns and melts and roasts every bit as effectively as Scorch's attack. The chains finally give way, crumpling to the ground. All that's left is an empty chair.

'Torch, you idiot,' says Cannonball. 'You've melted Mr Fabulous!'

'Not quite, popgun,' says an old voice.

We all swing around and it's Mr Fabulous, sitting peacefully on top of the fighter jet.

'You're free!' says Yesterday. 'I knew you would be.'

'Hi, girlie. Sure. I didn't want you lot thinking I'd been held captive by this bunch of evil clowns against my wishes. I only stayed trussed up until you got here,' he says, adding, 'Like those chains would be enough.'

'Huh?' Cannonball looks confused.

'Sink or swim, punks, sink or swim.' He looks around. 'Seems like you can swim. Congratulations.'

'You let yourself get kidnapped by the bad guys so that we'd come and rescue you?'

'That's right, Switchy. Scorch had been stalking me since I arrived. When he got together with this bunch of wannabe bad guys, I let them think they'd beaten an old man. Nice move, by the way, becoming a tank. That was clever.'

'Thanks,' says Switchy, looking proud.

'Liarbird, great lying.'

'Thank you,' she says.

'Ha! And nice honesty,' he says, smiling. 'Cannonball, you flew beautifully. Torch, you cut the power with magnificent timing.'

'Wow, thank you,' says Torch shyly, under his hair as ever.

'Yes, I have to admit I thought I was pretty good,' says Cannonball, chest puffed. 'Better than a clam.'

Mr Fabulous is looking at me, with a fatherly smile. 'And Focus, you were brilliant! I take my Triple A cowl off to you.'

I waver in blurriness. 'Do you mean it? I mean, you've always thought I was crap. You sacked me. You didn't want me in the team.'

'I never thought you were crap. You just needed some

prodding, son. You had to take your own path. You were so busy worrying about everybody else and whether you could be a leader that you had too much pressure to relax and perform. You couldn't find the time or space to believe in yourself.'

'So being crabby, and kicking us around, even sacking me, was part of some grand plan to make us better?'

'It's called "tough love". I told you I've been doing this a long time, kid. Look at you all now – you have real powers.' He glances at Yesterday. 'Except for you, obviously, girlie.'

Yesterday looks crushed. Mr Fabulous still has a nasty streak, I decide. Or maybe he's still playing his game. Tough love.

He suddenly flies into the air and floats down to ground level. 'Meanwhile, we'd better go see how my other project is coming along.'

'What's that?' I ask.

'Golden Boy,' Mr Fabulous says simply. 'You think I only came to Australia to nursemaid a bunch of start-up Heroes? You and he have a lot in common, Focus.'

'We do?' I'm stunned.

'Yeah, he also finds it hard to believe in himself. Today's the day for him . . . or else.'

We make our way out of the old museum to the street. Police cars are everywhere, the whole region cordoned off, and Mr Fabulous gives the Chief of Police a sign. She barks an order and police officers pour into the building to arrest the bad guys.

I look at the older, more handsome version of Switchy and say to him, 'What's this look you've got going?'

He grins at me with pure happiness on his face. 'You know what, Focus? I'm not trying to be anything. This might just be me.'

'Wow,' I say. 'How sure are you?'

'At least 194 per cent,' he smiles.

'So long, pimply kid,' I say.

And that's when Yesterday suddenly gasps.

'What?' Cannonball says.

'I can see it!' she yells, her eyes wide as she looks at Mr Fabulous. 'I can actually see the future!'

Then her face changes and she looks up.

'Uh oh,' she says.

GOLDEN BOY

AGE: 28 years old
HERO GRADING: Triple A (conditional)
KNOWN POWERS: ➤ Super strength
➤ Flight ➤ Bullet-proof ➤ Full suite
of super senses
KNOWN CATCHCRIES:
'The future is Golden'

CHAPTER 32
IMPACT

We peel our eyes to the sky and there it is, the massive meteor, looking bigger than a football field even though it must still be kilometres up.

Coming right at us. Hurtling towards us at an unimaginable speed. With no Heroes between us and it. Seconds until impact.

Numb with disbelief, I have time to think: Goodbye OK Team. Goodbye world.

For an eerie moment nobody says anything, just watching this impossibly huge lump of space rock speeding towards us. Cannonball takes his little sister's hand. Torch looks helpless. Switchy is clever, turning into an air-raid shelter, with a flight of steps leading to potential safety underground. But it is too late for that.

Me? I wonder where Mum and Dad are right now. Then

I turn to Liarbird, and reach out a hand that is amazingly solid, given I am moments from death. Her serious grey eyes meet mine and a lot is said without being said.

Could I actually be in love at thirteen years of age? It is unlikely but then again, it doesn't look like I'll be reaching fourteen. Feeling cheesier than the first time I pulled on my superhero outfit, I say softly, 'I umm, have feelings for you, Liarbird.'

Her eyes widen and I take the moment to reach over and gently tug her wig from her head. Ghost-white hair tumbles down, and Ali Fraudulent is looking at me, shock in her eyes.

'And I definitely like you, Ali.'

Then her eyes change and she says, 'You're a moron, Hazy.'

I don't have time to work out whether she is still in lying mode, or telling the truth, before a giant shadow covers us all.

Mr Fabulous seems to have gotten younger all of a sudden. His muscles, usually sagging remnants of past glory, fill his suit. Even more surprisingly, he snarls.

'Mr Fabulous, survivor of the Golden Age of Heroes, is not about to stand here on a suburban street, half a world away from home, and get taken out by some rock,' he announces. 'Look out, meteor! Prepare to meet a legend!'

And he takes off like a briefly young rocket, soaring to meet the simply humungous meteor that now pretty much blocks out the whole sky. It is as big as the whole central business district at least, but falling. Fast.

Mr Fabulous becomes smaller and smaller, until he is just a dot rising to meet this enormous shape. Then he collides with it, there is a brief 'urk' and he tumbles back towards Earth, out cold.

Cannonball lets go of Yesterday's hand and rises to catch the falling nonagenarian. Gently, Cannonball glides back to the ground and lays Mr Fabulous on the footpath. The old man's eyes flicker, roll, then blink twice. He is groggy but awake.

'That didn't go so well,' he murmurs. 'Not what I used to be, hey, kids.'

I'm too busy looking up to argue. 'There is one thing, Mr Fabulous. The meteor has stopped.'

The others join me in looking skyward, and it is true. The meteor hangs there, as though somebody has hit a pause button.

'Look!' says Torch, pointing a stream of flame to the heart of the asteroid. As the flame dies, we can make out a tiny, shiny, golden figure, with two tiny arms holding up the meteor. Switchy loses his air-raid shelter look and becomes a giant TV screen, with a camera pointing at the little figure and magnifying it on the screen.

'Golden Boy!' shouts Yesterday. 'I knew he'd do it.'

Golden Boy grins in happiness, making sure he holds the pose long enough for Channel 78737's remote flying cameras to get his image. His voice floats faintly back to Earth: 'No matter what!'

He flexes his bulging muscles, pushes, and pushes, and pushes, and finally, impossibly, hurls the asteroid back into space, the enormous rock lurching away to maybe one day threaten another planet and give some bunch of alien Heroes something to worry about.

Finally, Golden Boy floats to Earth, hugs Mr Fabulous, and even high-fives me and Cannonball.

'Gotta believe, hey, Focus,' he says.

Golden Boy knows my name.

'Well done, boy,' Mr Fabulous says to him. 'You've saved the world.'

'It's a good feeling, old-timer,' Golden Boy smiles. 'You remember what it's like?'

Mr Fabulous chuckles, but with an edge of sadness. 'Not a day goes past that I can't forget. Enjoy it while you can, son.'

CHAPTER 33
A HAPPY ENDING

*S*o, that is pretty much it. Scorch goes back to jail and spends a lot of time in his cell, all alone, blowing his nose. Scumm (aka Moonface) also gets sent for a long time to a place where there are lots of long, earnest discussions about appropriate behaviour. Golden Boy becomes the nicest Hero in the world now he's managed to finally save the Earth. He even drops by the OK Team's old scout hall occasionally, to offer tips and gossip about Heroes.

I still can't believe Golden Boy and I are friends. I've taken all the posters off my bedroom wall, in case somebody from the Hero world ever turns up at my house. It's embarrassing to be too much of a fan.

After one final celebratory dinner at the Vegie Bar – booked out for the night as a 'private function' and full of enough Hero freaks to make even the coolest Fitzroy types look twice had anybody been able to see in, and with Lurch taking a night off as waiter to enjoy being the Son of Mantis – Mr Fabulous finally flies back to Gotham, first class, guest of the Australian Federation of Hero Types. Soon after, he is named Honorary Hero Figurehead of the Heroic Hall of Heroes. What that means is that Heroes take him out to lunch a lot and tell him how great he was – and still is. He's one happy old Hero.

And me? Life's good. I just might have gotten the girl, and now when I look in the mirror, I can mostly see myself in there, unless I choose not to. School doesn't seem like such a trial any more, and I'm getting on pretty well with Mum and Dad, especially now Dad has backed off on the freak stories as a reaction to my improved self-confidence.

I got a letter from Gotham last week too, informing me that my Hero status has been upgraded to Level D, First Grade, which means as of now, I'm not a trainee entry level Hero but a fully fledged Cape.

And that, my fellow freaks, is what's known as a happy ending.

EPILOGUE

I'm sitting in my room one night, sketching out some ideas for a new cape, when a voice next to me says, 'You've done all right for yourself then, huh?'

It's Super Dead Kid, as pale and ghostly as ever, at the end of my bed.

I get such a fright I fall through my bed.

'Yikes!' I say, climbing out from underneath. 'Don't just turn up in my bedroom!'

'Why not?'

'It's my bedroom!'

'Didn't used to be. It was a market garden once.'

'Really?'

'Yeah, and the circus used to set up next door. When I was still alive, I'd wake up and hear the lions roaring. That was so long ago.'

I look at him. He looks sick and tired and miserable.

'Why DO you walk the Earth, Super Dead Kid?'

'What is this? A trick question? Because I'm dead, maybe.'

'But why you? Why aren't all the other people who have ever lived in Melbourne also walking around?'

Super Dead Kid stops to consider this. 'I do see the occasional ghost, but not many. Usually they're at train stations.'

'They are?' I can't help being curious. 'Why?'

'I dunno. Waiting for something, I guess.'

'Like what? And don't say a train. Is that why you're around? Are you waiting for something?'

Super Dead Kid is thinking hard now. 'I've never thought about it, but yes. It's as though I'm waiting for a moment. Not so much a big "Day of Judgement" type of moment. More like there's something eluding me, something I need to know.'

We think about this.

'Super Dead Kid?' I say hesitantly.

'Yeah?'

'What if − I don't know if I should even say this . . .'

'Go on,' he says. 'Trust me, I want to hear it.'

'Well, what if what you're waiting for is to realise you're actually dead?'

'But I know I'm dead.'

'Do you?' I'm gazing hard at him and I'm more or less in focus. 'Think about what that means. Because if you are really dead, like others who have died, you should move on. You're not supposed to be here, on Earth, wandering around. Other dead people have gone . . . I don't know where, but somewhere else. Maybe you haven't moved because part of you doesn't actually, really, truly believe that you are dead . . .'

Super Dead Kid is staring at me with his red-and-white eyes.

'Wow,' he says. 'Big wow.'

'It's all about believing,' I say. 'This is something I know. Repeat after me: I AM a dead kid.'

'You? You're not dead.'

'I said repeat after me . . . I AM a dead kid.'

'Oh, right. I am a dead kid,' he says.

'Louder!'

'I AM A DEAD KID!'

We stare at each other again. 'Goodbye,' he says.

'Really?'

'Yes,' he says. 'I know you're right. It feels different already. Thank you.'

'Hey, no problem. Good luck, wherever you go.'

He has changed from pale to transparent. He's fading before my eyes. I watch him vanish.

'So long, sucker,' he says. 'Hey, wow, you should see –'

And he's gone.

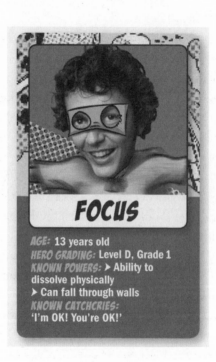

FOCUS

AGE: 13 years old
HERO GRADING: Level D, Grade 1
KNOWN POWERS: ▶ Ability to dissolve physically
▶ Can fall through walls
KNOWN CATCHCRIES:
'I'm OK! You're OK!'

THE OK TEAM 2: BETTER THAN OK

(LEVEL D, GRADE THREE)

Born a bit blurry around the edges, Hazy Retina's life as a superhero is going pretty well. As Focus, he is the Level D, Third Grade leader of the OK Team, a slightly less-hopeless-than-they-used-to-be band of still-pretty-bad Heroes.

But just as the OK Team is finding its feet, the bad guys – and several Heroes around town – find a mysterious new level of power and strength. Can it be true that a performance-enhancing substance, S.T.O.M.P. (Serum That Overly Magnifies Powers), is responsible? Does this explain the unnatural success of super-villain the Bushranger and his mysterious henchmen?

And what exactly is a Knight-hood Pact and why did Focus agree to it without checking the fine print?

Between dealing with the ethics of cheating and the increasingly erratic behaviour of his teammates (including new members Logi-Gal and the Gamer, who may be more of a hindrance than a help), Hazy a.k.a. Focus is up to his cape in strife. Will S.T.O.M.P. mean the death of the OK Team – and even of Focus himself?

Find out in *The OK Team 2: Better than OK* – to be released in October 2008!

www.herohints.com

ACKNOWLEDGEMENTS

*T*o Super Eva, heroic editor supreme, and everybody at Allen & Unwin for their continued enthusiasm and support.

To the various Heroes in my world, for support, inspiration and laughter. Including, in no particular order:

The Focstle Hero Collective (Ronnie Marvel, Wonder Jude, The Amazing M, Bellariffic and Incredoruby) and to my wider, wonderful family

Captain Shonky

Mademoiselle Manta Ray

The New York Tigress

'Hey, Winner!' And the rest of the Giants, past and present

The Canary

Miss Y, Queen of the Spirits

Sleight (aka Simon the Mysterious)

Mookie the Marvel

The Cat

Canvasback Stubbs

The Auckland Mau-auders (especially Blondie, and little Joel who, without even realising, gave me a straight shot of raw kid enthusiasm at the exact moment I needed it)

The Kingsley Hero Collective (Perth Division)

Super Goose

Shack Attack

And to all the other Heroic friends and family I haven't mentioned but appreciate more than you probably know.

And finally, to the creators and illustrators of comic books everywhere, for a lifetime of super-powered fantasy and imagination. Like Hazy, I remain convinced that if I just look up, at exactly the right moment, I still might see a human streak, or maybe hear the flutter of a cape. May I never lose that hope or that ability to dream.

ABOUT THE AUTHOR

Nick Place has been a professional writer for more than twenty years, in newspapers, magazines, TV, radio and the internet, but he refuses to grow up, regardless. Having worked as everything from sports reporter to comedy writer, he now runs a media company, ironically called Media Giants, and lives in Melbourne, Australia. His only known superpower is an ability to flatten surf by standing on a beach with a surfboard, ready to paddle out.